To Ann

D1475144

MURDER IN THE FAMILY

PAULA BERNSTEIN

*Hope you enjoy
This book about
a fellow Ob Gyn
Best Wishes
Paula Bernstein*

THIRD STREET PRESS

For Stephanie, in loving memory.

INTRODUCTION

Murder in the Family is the first book in the Hannah Kline mystery series. It is also the first one I wrote, the book that gave birth to the characters of Hannah and Daniel. It was originally the third to be published because it was the most difficult of the three to write, and went through multiple incarnations over a twenty-year period before I was satisfied.

Unlike *Murder by Lethal Injection* and *Murder in a Private School*, which are entirely figments of my imagination, *Murder in the Family* is based on a true story; the brutal murder in 1990 of a beloved friend and cousin. The murder wasn't a mystery. The perpetrator, who had recently been paroled after serving time for rape, was caught by the police, moments after the act, and put in prison for life. The killer had broken into her apartment in the middle of the night, looking for something to steal. In the aftermath of that event, in an effort to cope with my own grief, I spent a great deal of time talking to my cousin's friends and loved ones, collecting memories and stories. As a means of catharsis, I decided to write about her.

My first try was a psychological novel about how it feels when someone you've known and loved is murdered. I created "Beth's" fictional sister-in-law Hannah, a woman with her own interesting back-story, as my narrator. When I finished the novel, I gave it to my agent, who said she couldn't sell it. It didn't fit into a genre, because it wasn't complex enough for a true crime story and it wasn't a mystery.

A few years later, I added a few fictional elements and tried to turn it into a mystery, but I was unsatisfied. I had wanted to write a tribute to "Beth's" memory and this wasn't it. The novel went into deep storage in my file cabinet. However, in the process, I had created two characters I enjoyed, who were a good team for solving murders. So, I embarked upon my next Hannah Kline mystery, *Murder by Lethal Injection*, followed by *Murder in a Private School*. Both these novels made it to the first draft stage, but no further. I was occupied with a demanding medical practice, and a family.

It wasn't until I retired from my full-time practice in 2010, that I turned again to writing. I began by collecting and editing all my short stories and writing several more for a collection. At that point I took some of the material from *Murder in the Family* and decided to try to rewrite it as a short story from the point of view of "Beth's" ghost. The story was finished as *Joanna's Tale* and published in my collection *Potpourri*. At that point, I felt I had accomplished my goal of telling the true story and writing my tribute to my beloved cousin. This freed me to return to the Hannah Kline series. I did the easy thing first, editing and publishing the other two novels, and finally rewrote *Murder in the Family*, allowing my imagination free rein, and turning the story into a work of fiction.

CHAPTER ONE

"OKAY, HANNAH, YOU WIN," BETH SAID. "AFTER ALL, A girl's gotta eat."

"Twelve o'clock. The Pomegranate, on Main Street." I was grinning as I hung up the phone.

My sister-in-law had sworn she was handcuffed to her computer, but I knew better. Beth could always be persuaded to procrastinate, and I was desperate for some adult conversation. Much as I loved Zoe, my four-year-old, I was tired of discussing *Teenage Mutant Ninja Turtles*.

It was a beautiful California Sunday morning. I didn't hurry. I knew Beth would be at least half an hour late, and I'd long ago given up on being prompt myself. Zoe was learning to tie her shoes this week, and one thing she'd inherited from me was persistence. It would take a while before she gave up and asked for help.

In the meantime, I put on some blush and frowned at myself in the mirror. Whoever had invented *dress for success* hadn't been born with my hair, or for that matter, my body. My hair frizzed around my shoulders, defying me to run a comb through it, and to add insult to injury, I spotted two new gray additions to the red. My body was looking a little better, thanks to the workouts, but it was still a hefty size-fourteen. I changed to a clean T-shirt, sucked in my stomach, and buttoned my jeans.

"Look, Mommy, I did it myself," Zoe said, proudly displaying a perfectly tied sneaker.

"Honey, that's terrific," I said. "I bet you'll pass your medical boards on the first try too."

Zoe gave me a peculiar look and started on her other shoe.

———————

We were only fifteen minutes late, but we beat Beth, as usual, so we settled down with coffee, chocolate milk and the Sunday LA Times.

Beth breezed in, looking happier than I'd seen her since before her wedding. A youthful forty, Beth wasn't exactly beautiful, but she lit up the room. She had a long, narrow face with high cheekbones and exceptional green eyes. Long, thick auburn hair cascaded halfway down her back, held by a fashionable Gucci scarf, which picked up the colors of her yellow and purple outfit. The only blot on her appearance was her nose, which had been a match to Ben's, my late husband. Being a boy, he'd lived with it. Beth had submitted hers to the ministrations of a plastic surgeon, who'd given her a classic ski jump. Unfortunately, it had healed poorly and pointed asymmetrically to her left. I thought it gave her face character, and was still an improvement on her teenage photos.

"Aunt Beth!" Zoe said, dive-bombing onto her lap.

I gave Beth a hug and the menu. Eating with her used to be an adventure. I never knew what crazy food fad she'd be into next, but right now she was still in a Kosher phase. She'd started it when she got married and had kept it up, even after the divorce. I was tempted by the bacon and eggs, but settled for a jack cheese omelet instead. No point in being offensive. Beth ordered something vegetarian.

"You look great," I told her. "Is something nice going on in your life that you forgot to tell me about?"

She grinned. "I just met a new man."

I raised my eyebrows. Not only had Beth been celibate in the year since her divorce, she hadn't even dated.

"What did he do to catch your attention?" I asked. "Invent the human potential movement?"

Beth looked thoughtful. "I'm not sure. He's a new client. You know how, when ducklings hatch, they bond to the first thing they see and think it's their mother? I think my hormones finally got turned back on, and he just happened to be around at the right time. But don't worry, he hasn't even asked me out yet."

"Just remember, you're not allowed to marry anyone you haven't lived with for a year, no matter how fast your biological clock may be ticking."

"I know," she said. "I learned that lesson the hard way. What are you up to?"

"Same old," I told her, "Deliveries, hysterectomies, pap smears. I'm on ER call this week. Should be a bitch."

"Mommy, don't use bad words," Zoe said.

I covered my mouth. Working in the operating room, mostly with a bunch of male surgeons, had enhanced my vocabulary. I hadn't realized how much of it I was bringing home, until Zoe's nursery school teacher had tactfully mentioned that Zoe had been educating the rest of her classmates.

"Let's go," Beth said. "You guys can walk me home, but

I've got to work this afternoon. I'm already a week past my deadline, editing the Kingsley manuscript."

"Oh? And how many projects are you juggling simultaneously this week?"

"Only four, I think. I've got that new client with a mystery novel, *The Oat Bran Cookbook*, *The Woman's Guide to Holistic Therapies*, and Andrea's book, of course."

I groaned. Andrea Marcus was a good friend of mine, a delightful psychiatrist who, in her spare time, was writing a book on the psychological aspects of infertility. Unfortunately for Andrea, Beth had always subscribed to the last minute technique of getting things done. She'd fill her day with errands that gave new meaning to the word *avoidance*, and only start serious work when she was two weeks past her self-imposed deadline and her client was starting to leave obscene messages on her answering machine. Then she'd work a few all-nighters, and save the day. She always did her best work under pressure. Just thinking about it was enough to give me a migraine.

CHAPTER TWO

MAIN STREET IN SANTA MONICA WAS FILLED WITH Sunday browsers, in shorts and jogging suits, who carefully avoided the few vagrants from the homeless encampment on nearby Venice Beach. Unwashed and unshaven, wheeling their few possessions in shopping carts, they made a grim contrast to the yuppie festival.

There was a convenience store at the corner and Beth motioned me to stop. "I need some chewing gum," she said.

Zoe and I basked in the sunshine, watching the crowds and enjoying the day. Beth came out, backtracked a few feet, and handed a dollar to a homeless man sprawled in a doorway. He took the money and stared at us without an acknowledgment. He had a young, narrow, bearded face with hard, piercing eyes, almost the same shade as hers.

Beth turned toward me with a sheepish smile. She'd always been a soft touch, and I loved her for it, but my years of residency training in the county hospital had turned me into a cynic.

"Ten-to-one the guy's an ambulatory schizophrenic or a drunk," I said.

Beth shrugged her shoulders as we reached Rose Avenue, stared at the statue of the ballerina with the clown's head, and turned east.

Beth's neighborhood was in transition. To the south was the Oakwood section of Venice, one of the city's high crime areas. Just a few blocks west were the trendy restaurants, boutiques, and condominiums of Main Street. Beth lived on the ground floor of a seedy-looking apartment building. She had moved in a year ago, just before the divorce, and had been promising to invite us over as soon as the place was decent. As no invitation had been forthcoming, I assumed she hadn't finished unpacking, or had yet to acquire something to sit on. Usually, we met at a restaurant, or she came to my place.

The building had been built in the 1940s, and had probably been painted about then, too. It was a garish shade of blue with dirty white trim, and a front lawn that didn't seem to get either watered or mowed.

"Wait here a second," Beth said. "I don't have my keys with me. I'll go around to the back door."

She disappeared down the driveway. A minute later, she opened the front door and ushered us in.

The place could have been cute. The walls were white and freshly painted, the wood floors a light oak, and in good condition, but the clutter was overwhelming. The living room was uninvitingly dark, and I mentally installed track lighting. The kitchen had the usual assortment of unwashed dishes, and a tray on the stove was filled with freshly baked cookies.

"Try them," Beth said.

I reached for a couple.

"They're my wheat-free, sugar-free, peanut butter cookies. Pretty good, huh?"

I had already made the mistake of biting into one, but I managed not to wince. I really loved Beth, but I should have known better. I handed one to Zoe, and forced myself to finish the other.

Mittens, Beth's cat, a black and white tabby, came out from under the sofa where he'd been hiding and deposited himself in Zoe's lap. She petted him gently, a beatific smile on her face, and he started to purr. My refusal to get her a pet was a sore spot between us. I was barely holding it together as a single mom, and the thought of one more thing to nurture was more than I could handle.

"By the way," Beth said. "That B-E-A-R I was planning to give Zoe is in a plastic bag near the piano. As soon as I sew the arms and legs on, I'll bring it over."

The animal in question had been Beth's since childhood. It was about twice as big as Zoe, and Beth had been promising it as a birthday present for the past two years. Zoe's most recent birthday had come and gone months ago, but I wasn't counting.

"Are you sure you can stand to part with it?" I asked.

An expression of sadness passed over Beth's face, then disappeared as she glanced over at Zoe. "I guess I had some kind of fantasy about saving it for my own child," she said. "But at the rate I'm going, it's likely that Zoe will outgrow it long before any theoretical child of mine would be ready for it."

I squeezed her hand and she smiled at me.

"I was thinking of getting some new furniture. What do you think?"

"Great idea," I said. "I'll go shopping with you." A cleaning lady would be nice too, I thought.

"I really like the high-tech look."

Sounded good to me. Beth had never gone shopping for

real furniture. The stuff she had when she and Josh were married had all been his, and it looked like she had replaced it with discards from Goodwill.

"Are you sure you want to stay in this place, Beth? I'd feel better if you were living in a safer neighborhood."

We'd had this conversation before, any number of times. She'd always been adamant.

"I've been thinking about it," she said. "I keep hearing gunshots at night. The yuppies are moving in, but the junkies aren't moving out. I've actually looked at a few places in the Fairfax area."

I was pleasantly surprised. It was beginning to sound as if the old Beth was emerging from hibernation.

"Call me when you're ready to go shopping," I said. "I think Zoe and I should go now, so you can get some work done."

I gave her a kiss and detached Zoe from Mittens. Unfortunately, Beth wasn't the only one with a ton of work waiting at home.

CHAPTER THREE

Coming home, to my townhouse in Brentwood, felt like a pleasure. Emilia, my housekeeper, had no tolerance for clutter, and with the exception of Zoe's room, which always looked like the site of a recent bomb blast, things were immaculate. Zoe headed immediately for the television and put on a DVD of *The Little Mermaid*. I grabbed a Diet Coke from the fridge and settled myself at my desk in the bedroom, so I could dictate the histories and physicals on my surgical cases for next week.

The desk was a genuine Louis XV with a satin-smooth finish and inlaid parquet of dazzling complexity. Ben and I had fallen in love with it on our honeymoon in Paris, and his folks had shipped it home for us, as a wedding present. Ben's photo smiled at me from a silver frame next to the telephone.

Even after five years, it was hard for me to look at it without feeling a wrench in my gut and tears in my eyes. I missed him intolerably. He looked remarkably like his sister—the same narrow face and high cheekbones, the same slightly Oriental eyes and generous mouth. Ben's nose, however, was unmistakably Jewish and stood out from his face like a beacon.

We had met sixteen years earlier, during my first year at Harvard Med. I'd been at the Harvard Co-op, trying to collect the books for my first semester of classes. I'd managed to accumulate about thirty pounds of texts, and was balancing them precariously in my arms while teetering in the direction of the cash register, in my then-fashionable high heels. Ben was walking backwards in the aisle, perpendicular to me. Near as I'd been able to tell afterwards, he'd been watching some blonde co-ed with a tight ass, who'd been walking in the opposite direction. Needless to say, we collided and I landed ignominiously on my rear, my books flying in all directions. He'd been carrying something on the history of ornament, which wound up in my lap, from which I deduced that he wasn't a fledgling physician.

"Oh, God. I'm so sorry. Are you hurt?" he asked.

"I think I've broken a femur, but everything else seems intact."

He looked so stricken that I relented and smiled at him, accepting the hand he offered, so I could assume a more dignified position. What I'd actually broken was more serious than a femur. It was the heel on my new Bruno Magli's, the most expensive pair of shoes I'd ever owned. I'd bought them for myself as a graduation present from Vassar, knowing they were going to have to last the entire four years of Med School. I was devastated.

"I think I've got everything," he said, gathering my books and purse from the floor. "I feel like an idiot. You've got to let me make this up to you."

"It was an accident," I said. "But you could help me carry this stuff to the cashier."

He watched me limp into the line. "How about letting me carry those books home for you? My car's just outside, and you can't walk in those shoes. We could stop at the shoemaker's and get them fixed on the way back. At my expense, of course."

My mother had always warned me not to get into cars with strange men. She'd never said anything about whether I could let them repair my Bruno's.

"What's your name?" I asked.

"Ben Kline."

"I'm Hannah. It's really sweet of you to offer, but I'll be fine, honestly."

"If you don't let me make this up to you, I'll feel guilty for the rest of my life. I'll have to go into analysis."

That sounded like a fate worse than death. No one in Brooklyn, where I came from, ever went into analysis. Anyway, he was rather attractive. Some intuition was telling me that I'd be a jerk to refuse.

"I only live three blocks away," I said. "You'll lose your parking spot."

"Not to worry. I thought I'd take you out to dinner afterwards, so we'll need the car."

I smiled, remembering, and ran my fingers softly over the silver frame. Time to get back to my dictations. If I wasn't careful, my skills at procrastination would begin to rival Beth's. It had been so nice, finally seeing her happy and looking forward to something. I'd give her a call next week, and see if we could set up a furniture shopping date.

CHAPTER FOUR

A RINGING CELL PHONE AWAKENED DETECTIVE DANIEL Ross at two in the morning. He groaned and rolled over, squinting at the bright screen. The voice at the other end said there had been a murder in an apartment building just off Main Street, and he was needed. The call was not unexpected. It was rare for him to get a full night's sleep when his team was on first call.

He'd prepared by going to bed early, drifting off to sleep in the middle of a Preston & Child mystery novel. The book was still open, laying next to him on the blanket. He turned on the bedside lamp and dressed hurriedly, pulling on a long-sleeved T-shirt and jeans and retrieving his gun from the safe. He made a quick stop in the bathroom, splashing cold water on his face, brushing his teeth and running a comb through his tousled dark hair. His crime scene kit was already in the trunk of his car, along with a warm jacket for the chill night.

The address they had given him was only five minutes away from his Venice cottage. When he got there, he saw two patrolmen in front of the building and crime scene tape across the front door.

"What's the story?" Daniel asked.

"The next-door neighbor heard a scream and called 911. We were in Oakwood, dealing with a gang fight. When we got here, we found the victim in the bedroom, stabbed to death. The killer was gone. We secured the apartment, called you, the medical examiner and the forensic guys. When the backup cops got here, we sent them into the neighborhood, to see if they could find anyone suspicious in the alley or on the streets."

Daniel nodded. "Good work. Let's have a look."

One of the cops led him around to the back door.

Daniel's flashlight revealed no sign of forced entry. The door was unlocked. "Is this how you found it?"

The patrolman nodded. "Yes, sir. The front door was double-locked and all the windows are pinned. This must be how he got in."

Daniel put on shoe covers and latex gloves, and entered the apartment, careful to avoid touching anything. The woman was lying on her stomach, wearing a purple blouse soaked in blood, her slacks pulled down over bare buttocks. He wondered if she'd been raped before she was killed. He couldn't tell just by looking, although the posture was suggestive. The medical examiner would need to check for secretions or lacerations.

He could see defensive wounds on her arms and traces of blood under her nails. She'd put up a fight. Her killer had stabbed her multiple times, far more stab wounds than necessary to kill her. Arterial spray decorated the walls behind the twin bed and blood had pooled beneath her. The murder weapon, a large knife, was lying on the floor.

"Do we have an ID?" he asked.

"Yes, sir," the patrolman said. "Her name was Beth Kline. The neighbor said she worked from home as an editor."

CHAPTER FIVE

D ANIEL TOLD THE TWO PATROL OFFICERS TO CANVASS THE building, to see if any of the other neighbors had seen or heard anything. Then, he did a preliminary search of the apartment, keeping out of the way of the forensic team, which had just arrived.

At first glance, the motive didn't appear to be robbery. The computer, the TV, and the remainder of the electronics seemed to be in place. The dresser drawers were closed, as were the drawers to the bedside table. A large purse was sitting on a bedroom chair. It contained a leather address book, a set of keys, a wallet with several credit cards and $42 in cash. There was also an old cell phone, one that didn't appear to do anything other than make calls.

Daniel placed the phone, the keys, the address book and the wallet in an evidence bag. The furnishings all looked second-hand and the office equipment, including the computer, must have been at least ten years old. There were walls of shelves packed with books. He scanned the titles, which were eclectic and intellectual, not a single volume of popular fiction among them. She didn't seem like the typical murder victim.

Daniel was used to seeing dead gangbangers, prostitutes, and night-time cashiers at convenience stores. His typical case didn't involve victims who were young, attractive and clearly, very well-educated. Whoever broke in seemed more motivated to kill than to steal. He wondered what could have precipitated such uncontrolled rage.

The kitchen was messy with unwashed dishes and open drawers. One of the drawers contained a set of utility knives, which appeared to be a match to the knife in the bedroom. So, the killer hadn't brought his own weapon. That was interesting.

Daniel assigned several more officers to interview the residents in the surrounding apartment buildings, which shared the back alley with Beth Kline's street. Additional uniformed officers, who had been driving around in patrol cars, searching the neighborhood streets and alleys, came back empty-handed. He asked them to check into garbage cans and dumpsters in the vicinity, to see if the killer had gotten rid of a bloody garment.

Then, he knocked on the door of the adjacent apartment, to speak with the neighbor who had called 911.

A barefoot young man with messy hair, wearing a sweatshirt and pajama bottoms, opened the door. Daniel offered his credentials and the young man motioned him to come in. A woman was seated at the kitchen table, wearing a bathrobe.

Daniel could see that she had been crying. "I'll try not to take up too much of your time. I know it's been a difficult night. I just need to clarify a few points. What time was it when you heard noise from next door?"

"It was a little after one a.m.," the young man said. "Emily and I were in the kitchen having tea. We were getting ready to go to bed, when we heard this horrible scream from next door. I pulled the curtain aside and looked out, but I didn't see anything unusual. Beth's back door was closed. I thought about trying it, to see if it was locked, but I was scared, so I called 911."

"Did you hear anything else, while you waited for the police?"

"There was one more scream, and then nothing."

"Did you hear a door open? Or anyone leaving the apartment?"

He shook his head. "I thought about looking through the window again, but Emily was frightened and I was trying to calm her down, so I didn't."

"What about a car?" Daniel asked. "Did you hear the sound of an engine starting? Either out back or in front of the building?"

"I didn't hear anything besides the screams," he said. "The next thing that happened was a cop knocking on my door."

"Did you know your neighbor well?" Daniel asked.

"Just to say hello and to chat," Emily said, sniffling. "Beth was always friendly. Sometimes, the three of us would sit out on the back step and drink herbal tea."

"Did you notice anyone going in or out of her apartment on a regular basis? Friends, boyfriends?"

"Not really," Jeffries said. "Emily and I both work during the day. We mostly ran into Beth on the weekends. She was very religious. On Saturday morning, she always got dressed up and walked to the little synagogue on the boardwalk."

"I don't think she had a regular boyfriend," Emily said. "She'd just recently gotten divorced."

Daniel turned to Emily. "Can you think of anything else you know about Beth that might help us?"

Emily shook her head. "She was so sweet. Why would anyone want to kill her?"

"That is what I intend to find out." Just thinking about this murder made Daniel angry.

Beth Kline had apparently been an intelligent, and very religious, woman. Yet someone had brutally stabbed her. It was protecting people like her that had drawn Daniel to police work in the first place. He promised himself that this was one case he was going to solve.

CHAPTER SIX

MONDAY BEGAN AS AN ORDINARY, UNMEMORABLE DAY. Preschool for Zoe and a few elective surgeries for me. I planned to get home by late afternoon, in time for a one-hour workout with my trainer. If someone had told me, twenty-five years ago, in Brooklyn, that I'd actually be paying someone seventy-five dollars an hour to force me to exercise, I'd have committed them to an insane asylum.

The word *zaftig* was invented to describe the women in my family. None of us were endowed with less than a D cup, and our hips were cornucopias of abundant flesh. I have always enjoyed exercise about as much as migraines. *Why walk*, I always said, *if you can lie down instead?* My idea of working out was opening the refrigerator door, between chapters of a good novel. Nevertheless, the physician part of my brain insisted I couldn't spend my entire life sitting down.

When I got home, Zoe was helping Emilia bake cookies. I gave Zoe a kiss. Emilia, who weighed in at slightly under two hundred and fifty, and who probably still thought my exercise fad was insane, told me that dinner would be ready at six.

I quickly changed into my leotard and tights, greeted my trainer, warmed up with a quick two-mile walk, did squats and lunges with ten-pound weights, practiced bicep curls and one-armed rows, and finished off with sit-ups and push-ups. By the time I was done, it was after five.

I took a warm shower and shampoo. The phone rang while I was drying my hair.

"Hannah?" It was a man's voice, almost a whisper.

For a moment, I didn't recognize it. Then I realized it was Ben's father, calling from Connecticut. "Irving, how are you?"

"You haven't heard the bad news yet?"

Something tightened in my gut. "What bad news?"

"Beth was killed last night. An intruder broke into her apartment and stabbed her."

CHAPTER SEVEN

F OR A MOMENT, I WAS SPEECHLESS. IT WAS LIKE A BAD dream. I wanted to hang up the phone and pretend I'd never heard those words, as if I could magically erase the event by not hearing about it.

"No." The word came out of my throat, half-croak, half-whisper. "I don't believe it."

"The police came and told us this morning," Irving said. He sounded remarkably calm. Only the tremor in his voice betrayed him.

I didn't know if I could bear to hear the answer, but I asked anyway. "How did it happen?"

"She must have opened the back door to let the cat out. It was unlocked."

That had to be wrong. Mittens was an indoor cat. I remembered Beth's having mentioned that.

Was she raped? But I didn't ask aloud. I didn't want to make Irving think about it. What had her last few moments been like? It was every woman's ultimate nightmare, to be assaulted by a stranger, to have her body invaded by a hostile penis, to look into the eyes of her killer and know she's going to die. What had her last thoughts been when she saw the knife? Or had she been capable only of the most primal sort of terror? Was she killed instantly or had she suffered?

"What can I do to help?" I asked Irving.

"I spoke to the Rabbi at her temple," Irving said. "He's handling all the arrangements."

Arrangements. What a useful euphemism for figuring out what to do with a dead body.

"He's scheduling a memorial service in Los Angeles next Sunday," Irving continued. "We can't schedule the funeral, here in West Hartford, until the coroner releases her body. You could call her friends for me."

I couldn't imagine how he was managing to speak to anyone over the phone, even me. To lose his son, and then his daughter. How could he stand it? How could I?

"I will. I promise." I hung up the phone feeling numb.

I thought I should be screaming or crying hysterically, but I couldn't even stand up. I could feel water dripping down my back from my wet hair, forming a damp spot on the bedspread.

I had to call her friends but I didn't know where to start. Beth had a wide circle of friends, many of whom I'd met once or twice over the years, none of whom I knew well. Half the time, I didn't even know their last names. Someone was going to have to call Josh, her ex-husband, as well.

"Mommy," Zoe said, "I want you to paint me a giraffe."

"What?" I hadn't noticed her walking into the bedroom.

I reached for a towel, squeezed the remaining water out of my hair, and put on my white terry cloth bathrobe.

Zoe handed me her newest book, step-by-step instructions on how to make your hands look like animals, and turned to the giraffe page. "Paint me now, Mommy."

I let myself be dragged into the kitchen, where Zoe had set out her tempera paints and brushes. *Why not?* It would keep me occupied while I figured out how to break the news.

Emilia was making something Mexican for dinner. My mouth felt dry and the odor of food made me queasy. If I liked alcohol, I'd have gotten stinking drunk on a bottle of scotch, but I couldn't stand the stuff. I poured myself a sparkling water and proceeded to paint large black spots over both of Zoe's arms. She was enchanted with the results and insisted on photos.

Afterwards, I insisted on a bath. I settled Zoe into the tub with a large bar of soap, her submarine, and instructions not to come out until she was clean. Then, I closed the door to my bedroom, took a deep breath, and reached for the phone.

Beth's best friend in LA was Lisa Revere, a corporate lawyer with McLoughlin, Nicholson and Ames, one of the stuffier downtown law firms. I'd known Lisa for years, and I knew she'd be devastated. She and I, and Beth, had scheduled a dinner date for next week.

I didn't know of any nice way to say it, so I just told her.

I could hear her crying over the telephone, as I gave her the information about the murder. I could feel my own sobs trying to force themselves past my throat, but I still couldn't cry.

I'd been through something equally painful before, so I knew it would be awhile before the tears came. I was in my coping mode. I'd do everything I had to do first, then I'd break down and totally lose it. It was how I'd survived Ben's death.

Lisa knew a number of Beth's other friends and offered to call them for me. We figured, in a few hours, the news would be all over LA. I told her the memorial arrangements and rang off, so I could call Andrea.

I suppose, if anyone qualified for the dubious distinction of being my best friend, it was Andrea. Truth be told, she was my only real friend. Not that I'd been able to be much of a friend to anyone for the past few years. Between Zoe and my job, I felt sucked dry. Mostly I griped and Andrea listened, a skill that had made her quite a success as a psychiatrist. But Andrea had recently acquired a handsome new husband and an adorable baby, and was beginning to appreciate, first hand, some of the reasons for my own exhaustion.

I had introduced her to Beth five years ago, when she needed an editor to help with her book. The two of them had met weekly since the introduction, but I was convinced they spent more time gossiping than working, because the opus still had several chapters to go. They also shared a common passion for antiques, and spent many happy hours treasure hunting at thrift stores together.

I forced myself to dial and broke the news as gently as I could. I wanted to hug her, to console her and be consoled, but all I could do over the phone was listen to her cry. I tried to answer her questions, but realized I didn't have any information.

Who was the killer? Who had discovered the body? I needed to talk to the police, but I didn't think I could stand the details right now. I'd already learned all I could bear to know.

CHAPTER EIGHT

T HE MORNING AFTER THE MURDER, I WOKE UP FEELING
exhausted and agitated. I got Zoe off to school, drank two cups of black coffee, and headed for the office. I knew I needed more information, but I was dreading the process of obtaining it. It took me fifteen minutes, and lots of deep breaths, before I could get up my courage to dial.

The homicide department transferred my call to a detective named Daniel Ross.

"Detective Ross," I said, "My name is Dr. Hannah Kline. I understand you're in charge of investigating the Beth Kline murder."

Ross paused for a moment before replying. "Are you her sister?"

"Sister-in-law," I said. "I'm still in shock."

"I'm so sorry. Detectives are supposed to develop a tough skin to help them deal with seeing these things, day after day, but some crimes just touch you where it really hurts. Your sister-in-law's murder was one of them."

"Can you tell me what happened?" I asked. "How did he get in?"

Ross sighed. "There was no forced entry. She must have opened the back door, or left it unlocked. The neighbors heard her scream and dialed 911. By the time the patrol car arrived, she was already dead and her killer was gone."

"Did he rape her?" I could barely force the words past my throat.

"We won't know until the autopsy's finished," he said.

"I just saw her yesterday," I said. "I was in the apartment. My fingerprints are probably all over."

Why hadn't I said something to her about security? Why hadn't I reminded her to lock her doors when I left? Maybe I could have changed things. Maybe it could have been different.

"I want you to find whoever did this to her and I want him dead," I said.

"I'm in your camp," Ross said. "Anything I can do for you, tell me. I've got her address book and I can make you a copy. I thought the family would need it."

"Thanks," I said. "It'll help a lot. What about the cat?"

"We've asked the neighbors to look after him for the time being. We always try to make sure the animals are taken care of in these cases."

He sounded like a kind man.

"I really appreciate your calling. I'm going to need to meet with you," Ross said. "Preferably today. I'll need all the information you can give me on your sister-in-law. When would be a good time?"

"Can you come to my office?" I asked. "I don't want my daughter to see the police at our home. I have patients scheduled all morning, but I could make time at noon." I gave him the address.

"I'll be there," he said.

CHAPTER NINE

D ETECTIVE DANIEL ROSS HUNG UP THE PHONE, TOOK A
sip of his rapidly cooling coffee, and turned back to
the crime scene photographs. He needed autopsy results to
answer the rape question. There was obvious bruising on
her buttocks, but no clear sign of penetration. He'd have to
wait and see if the pathologist detected any sperm. Caring
about all the victims in his cases was part of what made
him such a good detective, but some tugged at him more
than others. If only the patrol car had gotten there a few
minutes earlier.

After the search of the dumpsters had come up empty,
Daniel had assigned several more officers to interview
neighbors in the surrounding apartment buildings. While
he was waiting for the forensic results, he requested a
printout of all of Beth's cell and landline phone calls, and
copied her address book.

He was planning to interview everyone in it, starting
with Dr. Kline, and proceeding to the ex-husband. He had
been a little surprised to hear that the doctor was in her

office. If there was ever an excuse to cancel a day of patients, a murder in the family would certainly qualify.

CHAPTER TEN

I PHONED RUTH, MY PRACTICE PARTNER, AND TOLD HER
about Beth's murder. After I spoke to Detective Ross, I
rescheduled my afternoon patients. I didn't know how long
the meeting would take, and I wasn't sure I'd be able to
concentrate once it was over. Ruth was surprised I had
made it in at all, but what were my options? Staying home
and crying wouldn't help, and work would, for at least a
little while, distract me from thinking about Beth.

The rest of the day went about as expected. Almost
everyone I'd ever met who knew Beth called, along with a
lot of strangers I hadn't encountered before. They all
claimed to know and love her. I told everyone about the
upcoming memorial service. One of the calls was from the
Rabbi's secretary, who confirmed the time and date, and
requested that I give the eulogy.

News of Beth's murder soon spread all over the hospital,
and other doctors started calling with offers to help cover
my patients. I decided not to be brave about it, and
accepted a trade for my ER call, with thanks.

At noon, Detective Daniel Ross showed up at my office, as promised, and my secretary showed him into my consultation room. Ross was about six-feet-two and well-muscled, probably in his forties, with a chiseled face, and eyes that were an unusually dark shade of blue. He had unruly brown hair, with a lot of gray showing at the temples. His face seemed kind, surprisingly untainted by the horrors he must see on a daily basis.

He shook my hand and seated himself opposite me. "I'm so sorry Dr. Kline. I appreciate your time. I know you must be very stressed right now."

"That doesn't begin to describe it," I said. "But I'll do anything I can to help you find the guy who did this. What do you need to know?"

"You said you were with her the afternoon before her death. Tell me about it."

"There's not much to tell," I said. "She and I, and my four-year-old daughter Zoe, had lunch at the Pomegranate and then we walked to Beth's apartment. Beth had moved in a year ago, when she left her husband. She seemed happier than she'd been in years, as if she was finally getting her life back on track. One thing that might be important is that she didn't bother to bring her keys, because she had left her back door unlocked. Maybe he got in because she forgot to lock it, before she went to bed."

"Could she have opened the door to let the cat out?" Ross asked.

"I don't think so. Mittens is an indoor cat. Didn't you smell the kitty litter on the back porch?"

"Good point," he said. "Were you close to your sister-in-law?"

"Very," I said. "My husband, Ben, passed away a few years ago, and Beth was the only family I had in Los Angeles. We spent lots of time together, both before and after Ben died, and especially this year, after her divorce."

"What is her ex-husband like?"

"A controlling, abusive bastard," I said. "He looks good on paper, and he's very attractive, but he made her life miserable."

"Did he hit her?"

"Not to my knowledge. The abuse was mostly verbal. Why? Do you think he might have done this?" I asked.

"We always look at ex-husbands. Did she have a current boyfriend?"

"Definitely not," I said. "She swore off men after her miserable marriage. She used to have lots of boyfriends. People were drawn to her because she was so pretty, and clever, and funny. She never lacked for male company and was pretty sexually active. During her marriage, she became an Orthodox Jew. After the divorce, she bought a twin bed and decided she would be celibate until she met someone who was really right for her. It was quite a change. I think some of it was due to her newly-embraced religious observances."

"What did she do for a living?"

"Beth was a writer and an editor. She worked for a small publishing company, that specialized in New Age books. She also did freelance work for authors who needed help with their manuscripts."

"Was she working on a book of her own?"

"Beth was always working on her novel, but never seemed to make much progress. She was great for other writers, but she had writer's block when it came to finishing her own projects. It always made me sad, because she was such a good writer."

"What time did you leave her apartment?" he asked.

"About four o'clock, I think."

"Did she tell you what her plans were for the evening?"

"The same as mine, work." I said. "She was behind on several editing projects, and she tended to be a night person. She got her best work done after midnight."

Ross opened a briefcase and handed me some papers. "This is a copy of her address book. I thought you'd need it to notify people. I'd appreciate it, if you'd go through it with me and identify as many names as you can."

The address list contained surprisingly few names that were familiar, and I realized how little I knew about Beth's life outside of the times we shared. I pointed out her parents, Lisa, Andrea, Josh the ex, and her boss. I didn't know any of the other names. I thought perhaps Lisa could identify some of them.

"Will you keep me informed, detective?" I asked. "I know her parents will want to know how the police are progressing."

"I'll do my best," he said. "I'll be in touch if I need any additional information."

Nice man, for a cop, I thought, as he left my office and closed the door.

CHAPTER ELEVEN

D ANIEL PULLED HIS CAR OUT OF THE DRIVEWAY OF
Hannah Kline's office building, and headed back to
the station to pick up Brenda Jordan, a young patrolwoman
who had recently been assigned to assist him. She was
smart and efficient, and so far, they worked well together.
He wanted her along to take notes when he interviewed
Joshua Meyer, MD, Beth's ex-husband. He'd considered
calling first, but after his discussion with Hannah, he
decided to just show up.

He had liked Hannah. She was extremely attractive, and
the look of anguish on her face appeared genuine to him.
At this point, everyone in Beth Kline's life was a possible
killer, but he didn't consider Hannah a serious suspect. The
victim's ex-husband was another story.

He'd looked up Josh Meyer online that morning. Meyer
ran a holistically-oriented family practice in the Valley. His
website, a touchy-feely affair, offered such services as body-
work, compounded natural hormones, a variety of food
supplements, and high colonics. Daniel rolled his eyes as

he read. He hadn't even met the guy yet, but he already had him classified as a phony.

Brenda was ready to leave when Daniel pulled into the station parking lot. She was a stocky blonde, with a no-nonsense short haircut and an engaging smile. She had a reusable shopping bag from Whole Foods with her, and as Daniel headed for the freeway, she offered him a turkey sandwich.

"I figured you didn't have time for lunch, and neither did I. I hate doing interviews on an empty stomach."

Daniel grinned. "Are you angling for a promotion?"

"Nope. If I had a promotion in mind, I'd have gotten you dessert."

"Thanks. You have no idea how cranky I get when I'm hungry," he said.

"I have a very good idea. That's why I picked up the sandwiches." Brenda consulted the Google map she'd printed out. "The address is on Ventura in Sherman Oaks. Take the first exit when you get to the Valley."

Daniel loved the way she was always prepared.

"How was the interview with the victim's sister-in-law?"

"She was nice, and helpful, and appeared devastated about the murder. Very smart woman. I noticed degrees from Vassar and Harvard on her wall," he said.

"Not a serious suspect?"

"I don't think so. I didn't even ask her for an alibi. I think she might be helpful on this case. I didn't want to anger her, right off the bat."

"What about her husband, Beth Kline's brother?" Brenda asked.

"He's deceased. She lives with her four-year-old daughter."

"Deceased from what?" Brenda asked.

"Didn't ask. We can retrieve his death certificate," Daniel said, as they pulled up in front of Joshua Meyer's office.

———

The Center for Holistic Healing was in a one-story building, tucked between a vegan restaurant and a thrift store. The waiting room was furnished with brightly colored plastic chairs, magazine racks and inexpensive poster art. A young receptionist, wearing a tie-dye dress, no makeup and a gold nose stud, sat at a counter behind a closed, sliding glass window. A few patients were scattered about the room, reading or checking their smart phones.

Daniel walked up, slid the window open, and waited for her attention.

"Can I help you?"

"Detective Daniel Ross to see Dr. Meyer."

"Do you have an appointment?"

Daniel presented his police credentials. "No, but I suggest he see me now."

The receptionist appeared unflustered. "Please have a seat. I'll let the doctor know you're here."

Shortly afterward, she appeared at the door to the inner office and escorted them to Joshua Meyer's consultation room.

———

Meyer appeared to be in his fifties. He was short and wiry, and gave an impression of perpetual motion. Light brown hair, with a receding hairline, liberally sprinkled with gray, was drawn back into a neat ponytail. His face was bearded, with handsome features and his smile revealed a mouthful of even white teeth. He was wearing floppy trousers, a white turtleneck shirt, and a dark linen unconstructed jacket with large shoulder pads.

He was standing behind his desk as they entered. "What is this about?" he demanded.

"Why don't you sit down, Dr. Meyer?" Daniel said. "I'm Detective Ross. This is my associate, Sergeant Brenda Jordan. I'm afraid I have some sad news for you."

Meyer sat. Daniel and Brenda followed suit. Brenda took out her notepad and pen.

"Your former wife, Beth Kline, was killed last night. Someone broke into her apartment and stabbed her to death." Daniel watched Meyer's face carefully, as he broke the news.

Meyer expressed the expected shock. He closed his eyes, covered his face with his hands and took a deep breath. Finally, he looked up. "I'm shocked and sorry to hear that. We were divorced, as you probably know, but I always wished her well. Do you know who was responsible?"

"Not yet," Daniel said. "Did your ex-wife have any enemies that you know of, anyone who hated her?"

"Everyone loved Beth," Meyer said. "She had a million friends."

"How long were you married?" Daniel asked.

"Five years. She left me a year ago. It was completely unexpected. I thought we were happy. I came home from a week-long conference, to find she had taken all her things and moved out."

"Did she say why?"

"She claimed I was too controlling but that was

nonsense. I only did what I thought was best for both of us."

"So, you were unhappy about the divorce?" Daniel asked.

"I didn't want a divorce, but she insisted."

"Was it a contentious divorce?"

"Not at all. We didn't have anything to fight over. We were renting an apartment. All we owned together were a few pieces of furniture, and she didn't ask for any alimony. It was a very quick, acrimony-free divorce."

"Really? It's unusual for a wife who is earning much less than her husband not to request support."

Meyer shrugged. "She said she just wanted out of the marriage and was perfectly capable of supporting herself."

"What about joint savings?" Daniel asked.

"There wasn't much. Neither of us was very good about saving. When she left, she used our joint checking and savings account to pay off our joint credit card, and then she cancelled it. There wasn't anything left to speak of."

"Weren't you angry when you discovered what she had done?"

"Of course, I was angry, but the judge said that she had a perfect right to pay off our joint debts with our joint money. I couldn't get anything back from her."

"I see. Was Beth your first wife?"

"No," Meyer said. "I've been married before. I have a grown son."

"Here in LA?" Daniel asked.

"No, he lives in Colorado."

"Are you close to your son, doctor?"

"I haven't seen him in two years. What's this got to do with Beth?"

"When was the last time you saw Beth, Dr. Meyer?"

"A few months ago, at the Rabbi's office, when I gave her a Get."

"A Get?" Daniel asked.

"That's a Jewish divorce. Orthodox Judaism doesn't recognize a civil divorce. A woman can only remarry if she has a Get. We're both very observant, so it was important to her to be divorced according to Jewish law. I haven't seen her since."

"Can you tell me where you were on Sunday night, between midnight and two a.m., doctor?"

"I was home, in bed, with a young lady. I'm sure she'll be happy to vouch for me," he said, with a smug look on his face.

"And the young lady's name?" Daniel asked.

"Amber Brennan," he said. "She's my receptionist. Feel free to ask her."

Daniel turned to Brenda. "Would you have a quiet word with the 'young lady' while I finish up here with Dr. Meyer?"

"Certainly, sir," Brenda said, as she got up and left the room.

Daniel asked a few more routine questions, giving Brenda adequate time to question the receptionist. Then, he gave Meyer his card and left.

"The guy truly is a creep," Brenda said, as they walked to the car.

Daniel agreed. No wonder Hannah had disliked him.

CHAPTER TWELVE

O N MY WAY HOME FROM THE OFFICE, I STOPPED AT A children's bookstore in Santa Monica.

"I need something on death for a four-year-old," I told the proprietor.

She pointed me to the appropriate shelf. There was a respectable collection of volumes on the subject: grandparents, great-grandparents, uncles, pet turtles and dogs. There weren't any books on murdered aunts. I settled for a volume about a little girl whose grandmother had died. At least, the gender was right.

———

There were few things Zoe enjoyed as much as a new book. I curled up on the large armchair in my room, and Zoe snuggled into my lap. "Maria began to cry. Won't I ever see her again? she asked. No dear, Mother said softly. She will be there in your mind, whenever you think about her, or look at her picture."

I held Zoe close and buried my face in her mass of curly, dark hair. It smelled of baby shampoo.

"Zoe, there's a special reason Mommy bought you this book." There was a tear dripping down my nose, but I tried to ignore it. "Mommy's been very sad, all day. Aunt Beth died yesterday."

Zoe turned and looked at me. "You mean, she's not going to come back?"

"No, sweetheart. That's what it means to die. You can't come back. That's why Mommy feels so sad."

"Read it again," Zoe said.

"Maria looked out the window at the moon and the stars. Maybe Nana is up there, sitting on the moon, she said. Or maybe, she's become a star." Altogether, we read the book ten times.

Then, Zoe went to the living room and put *The Land Before Time* on the DVD player. She fast-forwarded to the place where the baby dinosaur's mother dies.

"Is Aunt Beth up in the sky?" she asked.

"I think so."

How the hell did I know? I really envied people who could believe in God, and heaven, and reincarnation, and all that stuff. I'd seen too many dead bodies during medical school and residency, to be anything but a cynic. For me, death was final.

"When it gets dark tonight, we can go out on the balcony and look for Aunt Beth's star," I told her. "We can talk to her."

What the hell. One of us deserved some comfort.

CHAPTER THIRTEEN

E VEN THOUGH MOST DETECTIVES THOROUGHLY DISLIKED visiting the morgue, Daniel was anxious to pay a visit to the County Coroner's office. When he was in training, he spent a good deal of time observing autopsies. The science was precise and often supplied answers to otherwise puzzling crime scene findings. He also liked the pathologists. They were far less ego-driven than many of his colleagues, and they seemed flattered by his interest. He'd made a number of friends in the department over the years, and they were often willing to help him out by speeding up results.

The secretary told him that Dr Ian Scofield was in charge of Beth Kline's autopsy, and he could be found in the morgue. The morgue, unless an autopsy was in progress, always reminded Daniel of a freezing cold, college chemistry lab. One side consisted of six-foot-long, refrigerated, steel storage lockers for the bodies. The murder rate in Los Angeles being what it was, a body practically had to make a reservation to get in there. The other side had a large laboratory, with four steel autopsy tables.

The pathologists gowned and gloved for the autopsies. The entire set-up had the flavor of an operating room, except for the slaughterhouse smell, which took some getting used to. Adjacent to the autopsy room, was a pathology laboratory, where individual organs were sliced, stained, and examined under the microscope.

Dr. Ian Scofield was a pathologist Daniel knew well. He was a pleasant, balding man in his late forties, who had immigrated to the United States from South Africa about ten years ago. He had a very tanned face, with lines around the eyes and mouth that made you think he'd spent his youth on safari.

Ian was glued to the microscope and only looked up when he heard the door close. "Daniel, come in. Nice to see you."

"Thanks," Daniel said. "I'm here about Beth Kline's autopsy. She's my case. Is this a good time?"

"Of course. Just give me a moment." He made a few notes on a piece of paper, returned his slide to the wooden slide box, then filed both the box, and the manila folder with his notes. "Would you like some coffee? We can talk in my office."

Ian's cubbyhole of an office was meticulously arranged. The medical and forensic textbooks sat on his shelves in alphabetical order. The papers on his desktop were lined up, edge-to-edge. Daniel wondered whether he filed his socks by color. This was not a man who would have missed anything on Beth Kline's autopsy.

"I need to hear the details, Ian. Tell me what you found."

Ian nodded. "She died from a stab wound to her left ventricle. Her hands and arms were covered with defensive wounds. She must have fought like hell. We found blood and tissue under her nails, probably from her killer, so there should be DNA to match, once you have a suspect. There was a stab wound in the face, through the ear and out the opposite cheek. Of course, you saw that for yourself. The stomach contents show that she had eaten within an hour of her death. Vegetarian Mexican food and some peanuts. Most of the peanuts were undigested. The toxicology report was negative for drugs and for blood alcohol."

Daniel wondered why she had eaten so late. Where the hell had she been? "Rape?" he asked.

"Hard to say. There was no semen found in her vagina or anus. He might have penetrated, but not ejaculated. That's not uncommon."

"Anything else I should know?" he asked.

"Yeah," Scofield said. "She was six weeks pregnant."

Daniel did a double take. He'd taken Hannah at her word that Beth hadn't had a boyfriend, but clearly Hannah had not been well-informed. Either that, or she'd lied. He'd have to find out which was the case.

"Can you run a paternity test on the fetus, cross-checking with the tissue under her nails? I'd like to know if her killer also fathered her child," Daniel asked.

"Yes, of course," Scofield said. "It'll take a little while."

"Let me know as soon as you have the results." He walked out, thinking about the surprising development.

The forensic team had finished collecting their trace evidence. Now, he and Brenda needed to search the apartment again, for a more comprehensive picture of Beth Kline.

"So, what exactly are we looking for?" Brenda asked, as she carefully peeled away the yellow crime scene tape from Beth's front door.

"A better sense of who Beth Kline really was, and some clue as to who might be responsible for her pregnancy," Daniel said.

He handed her the keys.

Brenda opened the door. "To start with, she wasn't the world's fussiest housekeeper."

Daniel turned on the living room lights, but they didn't make the room any more inviting. "Either she didn't have much money or she didn't care about furniture. This stuff all looks like Salvation Army."

Brenda walked through the kitchen and dining room. She began opening the cartons on the dining room table. "Just dishes and glassware. Don't tell me she'd lived here a year and still hadn't finished unpacking? She must have a lot of dishes. Judging by the state of the kitchen, she wasn't fond of washing them."

Daniel opened cupboards and the refrigerator. "She seemed to have a pretty restricted diet. Everything in here is organic, kosher and gluten free."

They proceeded to the bedroom, where Daniel noted that Beth had a very large wardrobe and was behind on her laundry. There was nothing of interest in the bedside table or in the dresser drawers.

He saved the study for last. That was the room he was hoping would provide some additional information.

The study was completely lined with inexpensive pink plastic bookshelves. One wall, and a closet, were filled with file cabinets, and there was a large wooden table with the computer, phone, fax and answering machine.

The first thing Daniel noticed was that the red light was flashing. He pressed the button.

Sunday, 11:03 p.m.: *"Beth, it's Jill. Got your message. I was at the movies. I'd have loved to play for a while tonight. I can tell by your voice that you're stir crazy. Guess you went out without me. It's ten-thirty. Call me when you get in, or I'll call you later."*

Sunday, 11:10 p.m.: *"Beth, it's Alan. Just calling to remind you that we're working together tomorrow, seven-thirty. See you"*

Monday, 12:00 a.m.: *"Hi, hon. It's me, Jill again. It's midnight. I'm eating a pomegranate. Where the hell are you? Call me."*

Monday, 9:32 a.m.: *"Hi, Beth, it's Ron. I'm calling from New Jersey. Just wanted you to know I passed my Ph.D. orals. You did a great editing job on the thesis. Wanted to share the good news and thank you. It's nine-thirty Monday, your time. I'll be back in town next week. Call you then."*

Monday, 12:05 p.m.: *"Hey, what's going on? It's Jill. It's not like you not to call back. I can't imagine where you are. It's noon. I'm in my car. Call me. I'm starting to worry about you."*

Monday, 8:07 p.m.: *Beth, it's Alan. It's eight o'clock. Not like you to be late without calling. I even made dinner for us and it's getting cold. Where are you?"*

Daniel unplugged and bagged the answering machine.

"I wonder who Alan is?" Brenda asked. "Obviously a client, but maybe the boyfriend?"

"We'll find out. I'd like to interview him and Jill, as well as Lisa."

"Lisa?"

Daniel nodded. "Hannah flagged her as Beth's closest friend. All of them are listed in her address book or in her phone."

"I guess that's our schedule for tomorrow," Brenda said.

CHAPTER FOURTEEN

THE LAW OFFICES OF McLOUGHLEN, NICHOLSON AND Ames occupied the 24th floor of an office tower downtown, on Flower Street. Daniel had made a ten o'clock appointment with Lisa Revere. She didn't keep them waiting.

Lisa was a tall, attractive woman, wearing a beautifully tailored, navy-blue suit with gold buttons and a red scarf. Her straight black hair was cut in a chin-length bob with bangs, framing an elfin, Irish face. Blue eyes with long lashes, a snub nose, and a wide mouth accented with lip-gloss, completed the picture.

She greeted them politely in the reception area, and escorted them to her office. Closing the door firmly behind her, she motioned them to the comfortable chairs opposite her desk, from which they could appreciate the view of the San Gabriel Mountains to the North.

"Would you like some coffee? It's fresh," she said, nodding in the direction of a side table with a stainless-steel thermos and mugs.

Daniel accepted. He could tell from the set of her shoulders how tense she was, and thought she might need a few moments to compose herself before the interview began.

Brenda declined, taking out her notebook and pen.

Lisa poured a cup for Daniel and one for herself, which she placed on her desk. She held the cup tightly between her hands, as if to warm them, once she was seated.

"Thank you for seeing us," Daniel said. "I hope you'll be able to help us with our investigation. Hannah Kline told us you were Beth's closest friend in Los Angeles."

Lisa nodded. "I was. We met years ago. She was trying to write and I was trying to sing. The struggle gave us a lot in common."

"Sing?" Daniel asked.

"I used to have my own band, but I never got a record deal. Law is my second career."

"It looks like you've done well at it," he said. She looked like a lawyer, serious and strait-laced. He had trouble imagining her on stage.

Lisa shrugged. "It pays the rent, but you don't get applause when you close a real estate deal."

"Tell me about Beth," he said. "Were you close, even after she married?"

"I tried," Lisa said. "It wasn't easy. Josh was very jealous and very controlling. He didn't want her to spend any time with her friends or family. He wanted all her attention. It got even worse when the two of them joined that Orthodox congregation, a few months after the wedding. He decided she shouldn't associate with anyone who wasn't Jewish. Do you think he was the one who killed her?"

"We're looking into all the possibilities," Daniel said. "Do you think he was capable of killing her?"

"He certainly tried to kill her spirit. But, she told me he never hit her. His style was to withhold, emotionally and physically. To be honest, I can't imagine him getting his hands bloody."

"Did you see her more frequently, after she left him?" Daniel asked.

Lisa smiled. "We picked up right where we left off. We spoke several times a week, and tried to get together at least once or twice a month. I'd have liked to have seen her more often, but my job requires a lot of travel and Beth was working very hard, trying to hold it together financially."

"How did she seem to you, emotionally?"

"I'd say her primary emotion was relief. She was so happy to be out of that toxic marriage. She threw herself into her work and tried to reconnect with her old friends. She also stayed active in her synagogue. I assumed she'd leave once the marriage was over, but she wanted to see if her attraction to the lifestyle was real, or if she'd been brainwashed by Josh. She said she didn't want to throw out the baby with the bath water. If only she *had* left. She might have moved somewhere that wasn't within walking distance of the synagogue, and this might never have happened."

"When did she start dating again?" Daniel asked.

Lisa shook her head. "She didn't. She wasn't ready. Of course, she wanted to marry again, and she really wanted to have a baby, but until she understood what had drawn her to make such a bad choice with Josh, she didn't trust herself in another relationship."

"Would she have told you if she was dating, or even casually sleeping with someone?" he asked.

"She had always told me everything about her sex life and the men she met, before she got married. I have no reason to think she would conceal a new relationship from me. We trusted each other."

For a moment Daniel contemplated telling Lisa that Beth had been pregnant, but decided against it. Unless she was lying to him, she couldn't lead him to the father. "Can you think of any enemies she had, anyone who hated her enough to harm her?"

"Beth wasn't the kind of person who made enemies. She always tried to find the good in people, even people others might have found obnoxious."

"When was the last time you saw her?"

"A month ago. We were both busy, but the three of us—including Hannah—had scheduled a dinner date for this week. I cried when I saw it come up on my calendar. We spoke to confirm it, two days before she died. She seemed to be in a really good mood." Lisa reached up, and wiped the corner of her eye with her index finger.

Daniel could see she was barely holding her composure. "Thank you, Ms. Revere. I think that's all for now."

"You're welcome, detective. I'd better get back to work. I need to leave early today, to get to the memorial service for Beth tonight."

CHAPTER FIFTEEN

S OMEHOW, I MADE IT THROUGH TO THE DAY OF THE memorial service. I struggled all afternoon at my computer, trying to come up with something that I could say, in front of a few hundred people, without breaking down. I was certain there would be a large turnout. It was a tightly-knit congregation, and Beth's address book had revealed an impressive number of friends and acquaintances.

The Ocean Orthodox Congregation was a small, store-front synagogue in a shabby area of Venice that had recently begun to attract young families, newly-converted to Orthodoxy.

I harbored no warm feelings toward the congregation. Beth's wholehearted embrace of Orthodox Judaism had driven a wedge between us that had only begun to subside in the past year. I knew I would feel like a stranger in her synagogue, but perhaps that would have been true of any synagogue. I hadn't been inside of one since my wedding.

There was a large crowd gathered outside the entrance:

women in sheitels, men wearing kippahs and tallises. I scanned the crowd for a familiar face.

"Hannah?"

Peter Zach, the man I always felt Beth should have married ten years ago, was standing behind me. His thin, handsome face was haggard, his sandy curls disheveled. I fell into his embrace, and let him hold me for what seemed like a long time.

"I still can't believe it," he said.

"I know, me too."

Out of the corner of my eye, I spotted Beth's ex-husband Josh, wearing a mournful expression. I couldn't stand the thought of talking to him. If he'd been kinder to her, this never would have happened. Did he have the decency to feel guilty about how he'd treated her? Did he comprehend his contribution to all of this?

I returned my attention to Peter. "It's been a long time. How are you?"

Peter shrugged. "Apart from this, I'm great. I don't know if you heard, I got married six months ago. We're expecting a baby soon."

I looked around for someone pregnant. There were lots of candidates. "Do I get to meet the lucky lady?" Why couldn't it have been Beth? I thought.

"She's not feeling very well," Peter said. "She's not here tonight."

I nodded, understanding. I wouldn't have wanted to go to a service for my husband's murdered ex-lover either.

It was time to go in. I wanted to sit next to Peter, but it was girls to the left, boys to the right. The barrier between the sexes was so high, you couldn't exchange so much as a look. I walked toward the front of the women's section and sat down in the second row, saving two seats for Lisa and Andrea.

A group of authoritative-looking men were talking to one another at the podium. I asked one of the women to identify the Rabbi. She pointed out an elegant, gray-haired man in an immaculately-tailored Italian suit.

I decided to introduce myself. "Rabbi Blau, I'm Hannah Kline, Beth's sister-in- law. Your secretary said you wanted me to give the eulogy."

He turned, blue eyes evaluating. "How do you do?" His voice was cultivated, cold. "Are you prepared to speak?"

"I think so."

"Good. We have a program prepared. The press is here. We'll call on you." He turned away, dismissing me, with no expression of sympathy. A busy executive, staging a large corporate meeting.

The synagogue president brought the congregation to order. He talked about Beth, the observant Jewess and beloved member of the community. Several women in front of me sobbed loudly. Andrea, my best friend, slipped into the seat next to me and reached for my hand.

"Are you all right?" she whispered.

I shook my head and squeezed her hand tightly.

"And now," said the president, "I'd like to introduce Beth's sister-in-law, Hannah Kline."

Clutching my notes, I walked to the podium. "I've spent the afternoon struggling to find the right words to help you, and to help myself, mourn Beth's death, but as I sat writing, I realized that Beth wouldn't have wanted that.

"She'd have wanted me to help celebrate her life. In her forty years, Beth accumulated more friends, and a wider range of experiences, than most people do in ten lifetimes. She had tremendous intellectual vitality and an open, tolerant mind. She was a woman of many loves: her family, her friends, her community and her writing.

"Beth was a woman without a mean bone in her body. In the many years I knew her, I never heard her say a single harsh word about another person. I've had many opportunities to experience her warmth, her love and her generosity."

What more was there to say? My memories of Beth were intimate, private. I didn't want to share them, at least not now, not in front of a crowd of strangers. There would be a real funeral later, in West Hartford, for the family she had loved. I glanced over the audience, looking for more familiar faces. The only one I saw, besides Peter, was Detective Ross, seated in the back of the men's section. He caught my eye and ventured a small smile.

I took another breath. "There is no way to find meaning in her death. It was brutal, violent, and senseless. But there was great meaning and great love in her life, and I know that no one in this room will ever forget her."

I stepped off the stage, the picture of composure. I hadn't come close to breaking down. It wasn't my style to cry in front of an audience, and I'd already shed enough tears over the phone with Andrea. Lisa was sitting next to Andrea now. I had noticed her arriving, as I'd begun my speech. She touched my hand as I passed her, to resume my seat.

There were other eulogies. I didn't pay attention.

The Rabbi saved his speech for last. "This is an attack upon all of us—a violation of our community. The Bible says: 'An eye for an eye, a tooth for a tooth, a life for a life.' We demand the death penalty for the perpetrator of this crime. We demand revenge. Our community will not sit still and be terrorized out of our homes, and our place of worship."

It was a charismatic speech. I applauded the sentiment, but it was the wrong occasion. It felt as if he were addressing the press.

"Beth didn't believe in the death penalty," Lisa whispered. "She'd never have agreed with that."

I knew Lisa was right, although I was having difficulty with my own anger. Every time I thought about her killer, I wanted to shoot the son-of-a-bitch in the face.

Peter found me after the service, and insisted on walking the three of us to our cars. We didn't object. None of us felt safe in that neighborhood and never would. Three transients approached us for money, but we arrived at our cars intact.

"I don't feel any better," Andrea said. "If anything, I feel worse."

"I know what you mean," I said. "Sometimes a memorial can be a catharsis, the beginning of some kind of healing process, but this didn't help. I don't think I'll be able to even begin to let go, until they catch her killer."

CHAPTER SIXTEEN

T HE FOLLOWING MONDAY MORNING, DANIEL SAT AT HIS
desk, the contents of the Beth Kline file spread out in
front of him. It had been a week since the murder and he
was no closer to a solution. He felt frustrated and stymied.
The captain had just called him into his office, asking for
an update.

The Jewish community had used its influence at the
level of the City Council and the County Board of Supervi-
sors. Calls had been made by well-connected members of
the congregation. Parker Center had notified Daniel's boss
to give this case the highest priority.

The good news was that Daniel's team wouldn't be
assigned any additional cases for several weeks. The bad
news was that he was under the gun and had better
perform. Somewhere, in this pile of information on his
desk, had to be a clue that he had missed.

Beth's neighbors, and everyone in the buildings adjacent to hers, had been interviewed. No one had seen or
heard anything helpful, except for the next-door neighbor

who had called 911. Patrol cars had prowled the streets and alleys the night of the murder with no result.

Beth's computer had been an open book. She hadn't even set up a password to block entry, and all of her personal and professional contacts were neatly listed. Daniel had cross-checked them with her address book, and his team had interviewed everyone who lived in Los Angeles. Many were old clients who hadn't seen her in years, and were shocked to find out she had been killed. A few qualified as friends, and the alibis of all the males were carefully checked. Daniel had reserved certain interviews for himself— anyone who had seen her recently, and any male he suspected of a closer relationship.

Her newest client was named Alan Engel. He was writing a mystery novel about a serial killer. Daniel had read the first two chapters and the choice of subject caught his attention. He would see Engel this afternoon. Daniel also wanted to interview Rubin Krieger, Beth's boss. Given her fondness for older men, Daniel had him on the short list for the potential boyfriend.

The tissue samples under Beth's nails would yield a DNA specimen, but it would be a while before Daniel had it available to check against CODIS, the Federal database, or against the fetal DNA of Beth's pregnancy. The remainder of the forensics had been unhelpful. There were no fingerprints on the weapon or door. Most of the other prints in the apartment had been matched to Beth herself, and he suspected the few remaining ones would be Hannah's or Zoe's.

The dusty floors had yielded footprints, lifted with a new electrostatic device to Mylar sheets. They were found in the bedroom and tracked back to the kitchen, from which the killer had apparently entered and exited. He was wearing a pair of size ten Nikes. There were no tire prints that hadn't been matched to Beth's car, or those of her neighbors. There had been a few brown hairs, three inches long and curly, which seemed to be from a Caucasian, some blue polyester fabric fibers, and a soil sample in the bedroom, identified as beach sand from Venice beach.

As Daniel looked at the crime scene photos, he was struck once again by the number and fury of the stab wounds. The killer had gone on stabbing, long after Beth was dead. It was a crime of rage, and it felt personal to Daniel. He was convinced that the man who murdered Beth had known her and had a motive for the murder.

They'd looked through the databases for similar crimes. There was no dearth of stabbings, but most killers stopped once the victim was dead. The few crimes that resembled this one were domestic, and the perpetrators had been easily identified and imprisoned. There had to be some-where else to look.

He and Brenda would spend the next few days doing interviews, and then Daniel planned to canvass the local restaurants to see if he could figure out where Beth had spent her time before she was killed.

"Yuck," Brenda said, as she entered the squad room. "The things I do for this job."

He noticed she was wearing one of her interview suits, a smartly tailored black jacket with a straight skirt and sensible low heels. She much preferred slacks and a sweater.

She placed a manuscript on Daniel's desk. "I just finished this thing. It's got to be the creepiest, worst mystery novel I've ever read. The killer removes all the female body parts of his victims and all the police procedural stuff is wrong. I think it's beyond editorial salvage."

"The writing was so bad, I couldn't make it past the second chapter," Daniel said. "I would, however, like to meet the guy with the imagination to produce this crap. Let's go."

Daniel had made a back-up CD from Beth's computer and had called Engel's office, offering to return his manuscript and making an appointment to speak with him.

A Google search on Alan Engel had revealed that he was a Beverly Hills lawyer, but his office space, in an old building on South Beverly Drive, hinted that he was not a particularly successful one. After he and Brenda parked, Daniel intentionally left the CD of Engel's book in the glove compartment of his car. It would provide an excuse, if he needed one, to send Brenda out of the office.

The sign on the door for *Alan Engel, Esq.* indicated that he practiced alone, and the small waiting room, with the very young receptionist, hadn't been redecorated since the eighties.

Engel greeted them with a hearty handshake, clearly happy at the idea of getting his property back. Daniel estimated his age at about sixty. He was a tall bear of a man, muscular and fit, with a round face, and balding gray hair. His smile revealed excellent dental care, and his dark brows highlighted piercing blue eyes.

Engel dressed like a lawyer, sparkling white shirt, blue striped tie, and a pair of wool gabardine black slacks. A suit jacket was hanging neatly on a coat rack in the corner. The rest of his consult room consisted of a glass-fronted bookcase with a few law books, a large oak desk piled with papers and a laptop, and two cracked leather client chairs, which were comfortable despite their age.

Daniel and Brenda waited for Engel to seat himself behind his desk, before doing the same.

"I was so shocked to hear about Beth Kline's death," Engel said. "How can I help you?"

Daniel sat back, assumed a casual relaxed pose, and Brenda took out her notebook.

"Could you answer a few questions, sir?" Daniel said. "The more we learn about Beth Kline, the better our chances of finding her killer."

"Of course," Engel said.

"How long have you known her, and how did you find her?" Daniel asked.

"We've only been working together for a month. When I finished the first draft, I knew I needed an editor and I asked Rubin Krieger, the head of New Age Publishing. Rubin said that Beth, who worked with his authors, also did some freelance work. He gave me her number."

"Is this your first novel?" Daniel asked, keeping a straight face.

"Yes, it is. I spend my days doing bankruptcy law. It's tame and boring, so I thought I'd try to write something more exciting. Serial killer novels sell well. I figured, when it was finished, Rubin could help me find an agent."

"How did you get the idea for your plot? It's pretty dark. Guy murders his ex-wife, hacks off her breasts and uterus, and gets such a kick out of it, he keeps repeating the process. Do you have an ex-wife?"

"Very ex," he said. "We've been happily divorced for thirty years. She lives in New Jersey with her third husband. She wasn't the inspiration. I just read a lot of mysteries."

Daniel read a lot of mysteries too. Most of them weren't

nearly this gruesome. Maybe the ex-wife wasn't the inspiration, but this wasn't a man who liked women.

"What did you think of Beth as an editor?" Daniel asked. "Did you work well together? Your book seems very different from anything else she was working on."

Engel smiled. "That's what she said when she finished reading it for the first time. She'd never done a mystery before and I think she enjoyed the challenge. I thought she was brilliant. She asked all the right questions about my characters, their histories and motives. She taught me how to transition from scene to scene. She wasn't the kind of editor who rewrote your prose. Her focus was more on making structural suggestions to make the plot work better and the scenes smoother. We spent several evenings just talking about the book, chapter by chapter. I was about to start rewriting the first section, incorporating her suggestions, when she was killed. I don't know if I'm going to be able to do this without her."

"Did you find Beth attractive?" Daniel asked.

"You mean, did I want to have sex with her?"

Daniel nodded.

"She was very attractive. I'd have jumped at the chance of going out with her, or going to bed with her, for that matter, but I didn't think for a minute that she would have been attracted to someone my age. Anyway, if I made a fool of myself by making a pass at her, I'd have lost a good editor. Girls are a dime a dozen, but a really good editor is a rare find."

Slick answer, Daniel thought. "We appreciate your time, sir. Just one more question, if you don't mind. I wouldn't be doing my job if I didn't ask you where you were, the Sunday night Beth Kline was killed."

"I figured you'd get around to asking me for an alibi,

detective. I was out of town that weekend in San Diego, staying with my daughter and the grandkids. Came back Monday morning. I'm happy to give you her contact information, if you want to check it out."

Daniel took the name and number, and turned to Brenda.

"I left Mr. Engel's CD in the car," he said. "Would you mind running out to get it while we finish our discussion?"

"Sure boss, no problem," Brenda said, accepting the car keys.

They'd done this routine before and Daniel knew that she would do what was expected. As soon as she left the building, she would call Engel's daughter in San Diego and ask her what time he had left her home on Sunday night.

—————

"So, what did she say?" Daniel asked later, after he returned the CD and the two of them had left Engel's office.

"She said her father slept over Sunday night because he likes to leave after rush hour on Monday. It maximizes his time with the kids. She thought he'd left about nine a.m. It seems to me that, unless they planned the alibi ahead of time, we've hit another dead end."

"Maybe we'll luck out with Rubin Krieger," Daniel said, starting the car.

CHAPTER SEVENTEEN

"THERE'S SOMETHING PATHETIC ABOUT THAT ENGEL guy," Brenda said, as they headed to Santa Monica and the offices of New Age Publishing. "Hard to believe Beth found him attractive."

"She seems to have had a thing for older men," Daniel said. "Her ex was at least twenty years older than she was."

"Different strokes," said Brenda, as she pulled into the New Age parking lot on Colorado Avenue.

The reception room was certainly consistent with the overall theme. There were posters of Tibetan art on the walls and a Tibetan rug on the floor. The scent of incense made Daniel cough. The receptionist was a throwback to the sixties, with her long, unruly hair and Indian-patterned dress. The laptop on her desk was the only thing out of place.

"Reminds me of the ex-husbands waiting room," Brenda said. "I thought New Age peaked forty years ago."

"I'm not old enough to remember the sixties," Daniel said, "but there are communities that are a throwback to that time. Big Sur, for example. Even Santa Monica attracts quite a few people who were hippies back then, or who are much younger, but who idolize that period. Beth may have been one."

"We didn't have any hippies when I was growing up in Covina," Brenda said.

"We'd like to see Mr. Krieger please," Daniel said, approaching the desk and pulling out his LAPD credentials.

"Is this about Beth?" the receptionist asked. "We were all devastated when we heard. We loved her. Have you found the man who killed her?"

"We're working on it," Daniel said. "Is Mr. Krieger available?"

"Give me a minute. I'll go back and tell him you're waiting."

They didn't wait long for Rubin Krieger to appear. He was a handsome man in his sixties, slim and fit, wearing a pressed pair of black jeans, and a white linen shirt with the sleeves rolled up. His gray hair was curly, and his genetics had spared him from male balding. He had a tanned face with high cheekbones, a generous mouth, and prominent lines in his forehead and around his eyes.

They followed him into his office, which Daniel scanned, looking for clues to the man's character. There was a wall of bookcases, with books piled on them haphazardly. The desk and credenza behind it were covered in manuscripts, and there were stacks of paper on the floor. Clearly Rubin and Beth had shared a common tolerance for clutter. There were a few framed photos on the wall of Rubin with some recognizable

Hollywood celebrities, but none that Daniel could identify as family.

Krieger shook Daniel's hand, acknowledged the introduction to Brenda, and motioned them to have a seat. "How can I help you, detective?"

"Tell me about Beth Kline. How long had she been working for you?"

"On and off, for at least ten years," he said. "She was a superb editor. Clients loved her. Beth understood New Age, and was totally open to new ideas and concepts. She treated each client as if their book was a revelation."

"So, you knew her before her marriage?" Daniel asked. "Did you know her husband as well?"

"I met him once or twice. We didn't get on very well. He seemed very domineering, and disparaging of her work. I had the feeling he wanted her to quit working and devote her time to promoting his practice. She didn't, but I could sense the conflict. I was very pleased when she left him. She seemed so much happier."

"Did you ever see her socially, before or after her marriage?"

"Are you asking if we had a personal relationship? Never. I don't screw where I work."

"Do you know if she was involved with anyone else at work?" Daniel asked.

Krieger shook his head. "I don't pry into the personal lives of my employees, so I have no idea if she dated anyone, in or out of the office. You might chat with some of the others she worked with. She may have mentioned something to someone. The boss is the last person to be aware of company gossip."

"When was the last time you spoke to her?" Daniel asked.

"She was in the office the Friday before her death, working on the *Oat Bran Cookbook*. That reminds me, do the police have her computer and backup discs? We need copies of the work she was doing for us."

"The computer was taken as evidence, but the backups will be in the possession of her sister-in-law, Dr. Hannah Kline. I can give you her contact information. I'm sure she'd be happy to give them to you. One more question, Mr. Krieger. Can you tell us where you were the Sunday night of Beth's death?"

Krieger frowned, clearly insulted at being asked for an alibi. "I was at home. I caught up on a few TV shows I had recorded earlier in the week and I went to bed."

"Alone?" Daniel asked.

"Alone," Krieger confirmed.

"Thank you," Daniel said. "Now, if you don't mind, we'd like to interview the rest of the staff."

Daniel and Brenda split up and talked to everyone. The comparison of notes was discouraging. No one knew of a boyfriend, in or out of the office. Everyone confirmed that Rubin Krieger kept his social distance from employees. No rumors of affairs could be elicited from anyone. Apart from Krieger's inadequate alibi, they obtained no other solid information, and as Brenda reminded him, the hair found at the murder scene had been brown, not curly and gray.

"Now what, boss?" Brenda asked.

"Now, I spend the evening canvassing every restaurant within walking distance of Beth's apartment. I want to know where she spent her time on her last night."

"We could narrow it down by looking at restaurant menus," Brenda suggested. "Not every restaurant in Santa Monica serves vegetarian burritos."

"What would I do without you?" Daniel asked.

"You might have to do your own Internet searches," she said.

He laughed. "How did you get so good at it?"

"My dad encouraged me to take computer courses, over and above what they teach you at the academy."

"Was he a computer expert?"

"Hardly. But he was Chief of Police in Covina, and he recognized that the Internet was going to revolutionize police work. I'll never be as good as our IT guy, but..."

"But, you're much better than I am," Daniel said.

She grinned.

<hr />

When they returned to the station, Brenda did a computer search of restaurants on Main Street and Abbot Kinney, assuming Beth had walked, and expanded it to Venice and Santa Monica, just in case she had taken her car.

"You wouldn't believe how many restaurants there are, just on Main Street," she said.

"Oh yes, I would," Daniel said.

"I've narrowed it down. I eliminated anything that didn't serve Mexican food, and all the restaurants that close early on Sunday night. According to the autopsy results, she had eaten within an hour of her death. There are only three restaurants on Main that are a possibility, and one on Abbot Kinney, but lots more if she drove."

"Thanks," Daniel said. "I'll start with those. If I don't have any luck, we'll assign the rest of them tomorrow. Do we have copies of those photos of Beth to show around?"

"We do," she said. "Would you like company? I don't object to working late as long as I get fed."

"I'd love company," Daniel said. "And dinner is on the LAPD."

CHAPTER EIGHTEEN

I USED MY SHOULDER TO PUSH THROUGH THE DOOR OF the operating room, holding my newly scrubbed hands out in front of me. The scrub tech helped me into my gown and gloves. Ruth was already there, standing on the opposite side of the operating table.

My patient was prepped and draped, the huge bulge of her belly hidden, except for the window through which we would make the incision. I said a few reassuring words to her, tested the anesthesia with a needle, and said I was ready.

I used a purple marking pen to draw my incision, measuring meticulously from the midline. Patients were very fussy about the appearance of a surgical scar. The scrub tech slapped a scalpel into my hand. I took it, ready to cut, but my hand wouldn't cooperate. In my head, I kept seeing a knife and Beth's gushing blood.

"Hannah?" Ruth gave me a puzzled look as I stood there, scalpel in hand, paralyzed.

"Sorry," I said. I forced myself to follow the purple line,

mopping up the blood as I sliced through the skin. "Cautery."

The tech handed it to me and I used it until the incision was dry. I continued through the fatty layer, clamping and cauterizing each vessel. I didn't want to see or smell any blood. I divided the fascia, dissected it off the muscles and parted them, revealing the peritoneal membrane. Ruth and I lifted it with forceps and entered the abdominal cavity.

The deep pink of the uterus was exposed and I palpated the fetus's head, looking for the optimal place to enter. Pushing the bladder out of the way, I asked for the scalpel again and incised the uterus, layer by thin layer, until dark baby hair protruded. I didn't want to risk accidentally lacerating its scalp, so I extended the incision with scissors, protecting the baby with my fingers. I slipped my hand under the head and delivered it, followed immediately by a plump wet body, and a large gush of bloody amniotic fluid.

It was a girl. She started crying even before Ruth clamped and cut the cord. I handed her to a nurse and took a deep breath. The next part was always the worst.

I pulled on the umbilical cord and the placenta came out, followed by a big gush of blood. It smelled like a butcher shop. We mopped up, placed the uterus on the patient's abdomen to make it easier to sew, and started clamping the arterial bleeders in the incision with ring forceps. I tried not to look at the rack of bloody surgical sponges hanging opposite me, for the nurses to count after the surgery.

Get hold of yourself, Kline. You're a surgeon. If you think about Beth every time you're in the middle of a hemorrhage, you're going to have to find a new career. Do you really want to teach middle school or be a data entry clerk?

I reached for the forceps and needle holder, and closed

the incision in two layers. Once I'd finished, the abdomen was relatively dry, and it only took a few more minutes to close.

"Are you okay?" Ruth asked, as we left the room. "I was afraid you were going to pass out."

"I'm okay, now. I think I had some post-traumatic stress in there for a minute. I'll get over it."

"Are you sure?"

"I hope so. I'm going to head home and have some dinner."

I really needed to get this under control, I thought, as I was changing in the locker room. I couldn't let Beth's murder distract me in the OR of all places. It just wasn't safe. I wondered if the police had made any headway on tracing her killer, and if there was anything I could do to help. I'd always been a big fan of mystery novels and, at least in fiction, the clue to the killer was often found in the past life of the victim.

Perhaps, I could talk to Beth's friends. I thought I knew Beth well, but everyone has secrets. Her friends might tell me things they wouldn't share with the police. In the meantime, I needed to hold it together for the rest of the week, at least until Saturday. Zoe and I were flying East for the real funeral. Maybe, I'd function better when it was over.

CHAPTER NINETEEN

I N SANTA MONICA, DANIEL AND BRENDA STARTED AT seven p.m., to make certain they would catch any employee who normally worked the night shift. They treated themselves to a very good burger and fries, at the first restaurant they tried. At each place, they asked for the manager, presented Daniel's credentials, and interviewed every employee who had worked there for the past month. Beth's photograph was met by looks of polite bemusement. No one recognized it.

The third place they tried was C.J.'s, a large, noisy room with inexpensive food, that tended to appeal to a younger, less yuppie crowd. By this time, it was close to nine-o'clock and the density of people, as well as the noise level, was starting to get on Daniel's nerves.

They elbowed their way to the bar and ordered two cokes from the bartender, a cute young guy with curly brown hair and a bedraggled mustache.

"I'd like to speak to the manager," Daniel told him.

"Not here tonight," he said. "Can I help you? My name's Sam."

"Maybe," Daniel said. "How long have you worked here?"

"Almost a year," Sam said.

Daniel identified himself and Brenda pulled Beth's pictures from her purse.

"We're trying to trace the movements of a young woman, who may have been here a week ago. Could you look at these and see if you recognize her?"

Sam opened a bottle of Coors for the guy sitting next to Brenda, and then looked at the photos.

"Oh, yeah. That's Beth. She's a regular. Likes the vegetarian food. Is something wrong?"

"She was murdered about two weeks ago, on a Sunday night. Didn't you see it in the papers?"

Sam's eyes widened, but Daniel couldn't detect any trace of anxiety or guilt in his expression or his posture.

"I try to avoid the news," Sam said. "It's always bad, and you've just proved my point. I'm really sorry. She seemed like a sweet woman."

"How well did you know her?" Brenda asked.

"I only had one real conversation with her. Come to think of it, it was on a Sunday night. It was real quiet. Not much action at the bar. She had something to eat, over at one of the tables, then she came up to the counter and ordered some sparkling water. We started chatting. Turns out, she was an editor. I'm a writer, when I'm not bartending. We talked for quite a while. I even took her card. I was planning to call her."

"Do you happen to remember what time she left?" Daniel asked.

He nodded. "This guy came in, about 12:45 a.m., and sat next to her at the bar. He was young and grungy-looking, and I could tell he made her nervous."

"Did he say anything to her?"

"I think he tried to pick her up. Offered to buy her a drink, or some other original line like that."

"What did she do?"

"She seemed real uptight. I think she just said 'no, thank you.' Then, he asked her what her name was."

"Did she tell him?" Daniel asked.

"I don't think so," he said. "She just ignored him, paid her bill, and asked me where the ladies room was." Sam pointed behind Daniel, and he swiveled in his seat, spotting the sign, not far from the front door.

"Then what?" Daniel said.

"The guy gave me a look, said something about a snotty bitch, finished his beer and left. A few minutes later, I saw her come out of the ladies room and leave."

"Do you know if she walked home, or if she came here by car? It's about a six-block walk to her apartment," Daniel said.

Sam shook his head. "I'm sorry. I don't know. If I was a single woman and out that late, I'd take my car."

"Me too," said Brenda.

"Can you describe the guy?" Daniel asked.

"I think he was young, maybe twenty or so, shaggy, oily brown hair, Caucasian. Tall and skinny. That's all I remember."

"Can you remember what he was wearing?"

Sam pursed his lips, drawing his brows together. "Nothing special. Jeans, I think, and a dark jacket, black or navy. Hard to pin down with the low lights in the restaurant."

"Was the jacket a hoodie?"

Sam shook his head. "More like a windbreaker."

Daniel thought about the blue polyester fabric found at the scene.

"How late did you work that night?" Daniel asked.

"We close at 1:30. By the time we finished cleaning up, it was close to 2:00 a.m."

"Where did you go then?" Daniel asked.

"Home to bed. I'm usually pretty tired by the end of a late shift."

Daniel handed Sam his card. "I need you to come to the station tomorrow. I want you to look through some photo books and maybe work with our police artist. See if we can get a better handle on what the guy looked like. Try to think hard about him. Maybe some more details will come up."

"Well, that was interesting," Brenda said, as they walked to their car. "I sure would like a DNA specimen on the bartender. Think he was telling the truth?"

"He didn't have to tell us anything," Daniel said. "He could have just denied knowing her."

"That would have been easier, but maybe he's a killer who gets his kicks out of playing games with the police."

"Let's see what he comes up with tomorrow. At the moment, I don't see a motive for murder, but the guy with brown hair and blue jacket interests me."

CHAPTER TWENTY

T HE FOLLOWING SATURDAY MORNING, ZOE AND I FLEW to Connecticut. Jeremy, one of Beth's younger twin brothers, put us up at his house. He had a sweet young wife, and a three-year-old daughter for Zoe to play with, which solved the babysitting problem. Jared was the other twin. He was single, and Beth had always described him as her playboy brother. I'd met the twins when Ben and I were dating, and they were pimply adolescents. Now they were thirty and ran Irving's successful insurance agency.

We assembled at noon on Sunday, at my in-laws' home, for the drive to the cemetery. Irving, Beth's father, had decided on a brief graveside service for just immediate family and close friends—immediate family consisting of some sixty aunts, uncles and grown children. The family faces were all familiar but a hell of a lot older. I hadn't seen most of them since my wedding, fifteen years ago. Most of them hadn't made it to Ben's funeral, which had been in Los Angeles.

Oh, Ben, my love, why aren't you here when I really need you?

My father-in-law spotted me and motioned me over. I hugged him hard and looked for Evelyn, my mother-in-law. She was surrounded by a group of her sisters, staring vacantly into space, her face shriveled and a hundred years older. I tried to navigate my way toward her, but the crowd separated us.

I felt Jeremy's hand on my arm. "Dad wants us to start getting into the cars," he said. "You're with me in the second limousine."

Jeremy held the car door open, then slid in beside me.

"Dad said you were the last of us to see Beth," Jeremy said.

"We had lunch, the day she died," I said. I didn't really want to talk about it.

"I feel so guilty. Jared and I never bothered to visit her in LA. We were always too busy with our own stuff. I hadn't spoken to her in weeks. Jared feels even worse. He'd gone to Vegas for a long weekend, just before she died, and hadn't even called her."

I reached over and squeezed his hand. There was nothing helpful I could say.

The cars dropped us off at the graveyard, and I could see a white tent set up in the distance. As I was trying to figure out the shortest route, I spied Marsha Blinderman. Marsha was Beth's oldest childhood friend. She'd called me at the office as soon as she'd heard, a half-hour long international call that did nothing to soothe the pain for either of us.

Marsha had married an Israeli at the age of twenty-two, and was living in Tel Aviv. She and Beth had spoken at least weekly, for the past eighteen years. If this had devastated me, I couldn't conceive of how she must be feeling. Marsha probably knew more about Beth's past than anyone. At some point, I wanted to have a long talk with her, but today wasn't the day.

The phrase that always comes to mind when I try to describe Marsha Blinderman is *Earth Mother*. Maybe it's because she has four kids. Marsha is a large woman—generous breasts, wide hips and a constant struggle with midriff bulge—which gave us a lot in common. She'd moved to West Hartford from New York when she was ten, and still retained that New York Yiddish intonation to her speech, that I'd worked so hard to get rid of in mine. She had a plump, rather plain face, which changed to beautiful when she smiled, and great taste in clothes.

"We almost didn't make it," she said. "We had a flat tire on the thruway and had to hitch a ride with a guy in a VW van."

"You look great," I said, as I hugged her, admiring her outfit.

"I bought this yesterday," she said. "Beth would have wanted me to look my best at her funeral."

She probably would have. Beth had always had a weakness for clothes.

"Any news?" she asked. "Has there been an arrest?"

I shook my head.

By the time Marsha and I reached the tent, it was standing room only. The rabbi had known Beth since she started Hebrew School at the age of ten, and he sounded sincere and appropriate. Beth's body was in a simple wood coffin, suspended on pulleys above the six-foot-long wound in the earth. I could hardly stand to look at it. It reminded me too much of Ben's.

"We will now consign Beth Kline's earthly remains to her final resting place," the rabbi said. "Those of her friends and family who wish to help bury her, please line up on the left side."

The pulleys started to creak and the coffin began to descend. I couldn't believe, wouldn't believe, she was really in that box. The tears started to flow, a small trickle at first, and then my whole body started to shake. Marsha was sobbing too, and we held one another as if we were drowning. It was all right to cry now. I was safe. Everyone here would understand.

Jeremy covered the coffin with the first shovel full of earth. Jared, his twin, followed, then assorted aunts and uncles. Marsha and I held hands and waited our turn. Then, we wiped our eyes and headed back toward the limousine.

I wanted to be able to go home and start healing. That was what funerals were supposed to be for, but I knew that, for me, the worst wasn't over. It was barely beginning. I'd spoken to Irving that morning, and he'd asked me, as I knew he would, to pack up Beth's apartment.

CHAPTER TWENTY-ONE

Zoe and I flew back home on Monday, to a polluted, smoggy day that matched my mood. I'd told the office I wouldn't be in until Tuesday, so I spent Monday afternoon assessing the security of my condominium.

I hadn't worried about it much, until now. Brentwood wasn't exactly the center of gang warfare. I had double-cylinder locks on both doors and pins on the windows, but so had Beth. Her friends had all said the same thing, that she'd been careless about locking her door. I'd seen it myself, the day we'd visited. The whole time Zoe and I were there, the front door was ajar to let in fresh air and cool the stuffy living room. If her killer had been stalking her in the afternoon, Zoe and I could also have been his victims. I shuddered to think about it.

Beth hadn't died from lack of door locks; she'd died from not using them. Still, I'd had nightmares all week about someone breaking in and killing Zoe. I was tired of waking up with my heart pounding, listening for stray sounds.

I called Safe-T Security Systems, and three thousand

dollars later I had arranged to wire all my doors and windows, and to install a sophisticated system of beams and audio discriminators. The system came with patrol service and armed response.

I gave serious consideration to a gun. People say not to get one unless you're prepared to use it. I didn't have any trouble with that. In defense of Zoe, or myself, I wouldn't hesitate for a moment to blow some scumbag to kingdom come. I just couldn't solve the basic logistical problem. A loaded gun, within easy reach if I needed it, was also going to be accessible to Zoe. I'd heard about enough cases over the years, in which kids accidentally killed themselves or their playmates. If I kept it unloaded and locked away, I could be dead by the time I got hold of it. I couldn't seem to come up with a good solution. I wondered how cops with kids handled their firearms. That question reminded me to call Detective Ross and find out how to get Beth's keys.

"I was just about to call you," he said, his voice warm over the phone. "I have a few more questions."

"When can I start packing up the apartment?" I asked.

"Whenever you want. We're done with the forensic work," he said. "The keys are with the public administrator. I'll give her office a call, and find out when I can get them. If you like, I can meet you at Beth's place. It might be easier to have a friendly face with you, the first time you go in there."

I didn't want to impose, but the thought of having an armed cop with me in the apartment was appealing. I was terrified of what I knew I was going to see. Both Lisa and Andrea had offered to help me with the packing, but I couldn't let either of them into the apartment until I'd cleaned up. I was expecting a hell of a bloody mess.

"Thanks for the offer, detective. I would appreciate your being there."

"No problem," he said. "I'll call you later and we can find a day and time."

CHAPTER TWENTY-TWO

DANIEL HUNG UP THE PHONE, LOOKED UP THE NUMBER for the public administrator and checked his schedule. He arranged to get the keys the next day, and set up a Friday morning rendezvous with Hannah. Then, he called and made an appointment with Rabbi Blau. He had the impression that the Rabbi had his finger on the pulse of his small congregation, and that was an avenue he had yet to pursue, looking for suspects.

Sam, the bartender at C.J.'s, came in as promised that afternoon. Daniel gave him a photo book of gang members and wanted felons to review, to see if any of the faces matched the man who had hit on Beth at the bar.

He perused it slowly and thoroughly, and finally, after an hour shook his head. "They're all starting to look the same to me, detective, but I didn't see anyone who resembled the guy in the bar."

Daniel nodded. It was what he had expected. He introduced Sam to the police artist and the two of them set to work.

The sketch was more specific than usual. The face was

young and narrow with high cheekbones and slightly slanted, light eyes. There was a full head of wavy, unkempt hair, a wide mouth and a cleft chin. It was a handsome face, but something about the eyes was cold.

"Do you recall his eye color?" Daniel asked Sam.

"I wasn't paying that much attention. All I remember is that they weren't brown. Could have been blue, or green, or hazel. I just had an impression that they were light."

Daniel reached over and shook Sam's hand. "I appreciate all your time. You've been very helpful."

Sam shrugged. He looked a little embarrassed. "Yeah, sure. No problem. I hope you get the guy. Beth didn't deserve what happened."

After he left, Daniel had the sketch copied and sent to his team. "Start at C.J.'s and work out in a spiral. Show this picture at every restaurant, store, hotel, homeless shelter, and church in the neighborhood. There was beach sand in the bedroom, so cover the entire Venice boardwalk. We need to identify this guy and bring him in for questioning."

On Wednesday morning, Daniel and Brenda returned to the Venice Shul to see the rabbi. Brenda had put on a tailored pantsuit for the occasion, rather than her usual jeans. Judging by the wardrobe choices Daniel had observed at the memorial service, he suspected that the rabbi still wouldn't approve, but he wisely decided not to mention it.

Daniel had taken an instant, and perhaps unreasonable, dislike to Rabbi Blau at the memorial service. The guy seemed to be putting on a performance rather than demonstrating any real compassion. The rabbi struck him as a domineering cold fish, but he was willing to keep an open mind.

The rabbi's handshake did little to dispel his initial impression. It was limp and disinterested. He barely acknowledged the introduction to Sergeant Brenda Jordan and didn't offer his hand. Daniel recalled reading somewhere that Orthodox men never touched women to whom they weren't married. Brenda ignored the snub, seated herself, and took out her notebook.

"Why are you here, detective?" the rabbi asked.

"To ask you about Beth Kline. I believe she was a member of your congregation. I assume you knew her well."

"I did, but what has that got to do with finding her killer?"

"It helps to know about the life and contacts of the victim. Sometimes, it leads us to a person with a motive to kill."

"It was probably one of those Oakwood gang members. There are enough of them in the neighborhood," Blau said.

"We're considering all the possibilities," Daniel said. "How long had you known Beth?"

"She and her husband came to services about five years ago. When new people show an interest in the congregation, one of our members always brings them home for a Shabbat lunch. That way we can get to know them, assess whether their interest in us is genuine, and whether we should encourage them to continue to attend."

"And were they genuinely interested?"

"Very much so. Beth came from a secular background and knew very little about Jewish ritual, but she had an open mind. She asked complex and insightful questions, and once they had decided to join us, she embraced the community fully."

"What do you mean by that?" Daniel asked.

"We have a unique community here, detective. What we are trying to do is to replicate the kind of life Jews had in the shtetls in Eastern Europe before World War One. Our members have purchased homes in an enclave within walking distance of the synagogue. All of us keep kosher and go to services regularly. We have a Jewish school for the children. We function as a community. When someone is sick, or has just given birth, the women get together and make sure that household is supplied with meals. The men do business together. As the rabbi, I make all major decisions that affect the community, and its members consult me about all of their life problems."

"So, your word is law?"

"You could say that," Blau said. "It makes for a well-ordered life. Everyone knows the rules and abides by them. Everyone can count on the support of their neighbors."

"How did Beth fit in?" Daniel asked.

"As I said, she embraced the lifestyle fully. She became kosher, and followed the rules down to the last detail. She started dressing appropriately in long skirts and covered her hair. She came to shul regularly and read religious literature in great detail. She and her husband rented a house close by."

"And her ex-husband, how did he fit in?"

"Not as well," Blau said. "He was pompous and opinionated. His views were often different from our views. I had to apply great pressure on him, to get him to agree to give Beth a Jewish divorce."

"I see," said Daniel. "Was there anyone who disliked her

or resented her? Did she have any enemies in the congregation?"

Blau bristled. "Of course not. Are you implying that someone in our congregation could have been responsible for her murder?"

"Not at all, Rabbi. I'm just trying to get a full picture. After she left her husband, did she date anyone in the congregation?"

"Absolutely not. I would not have permitted her to date anyone until she obtained her Jewish divorce. Then, when she was ready, we would have found men for her who were appropriate potential husbands."

"And did you?" Daniel asked.

"No. She didn't ask me to. I assumed she wasn't ready to consider remarriage yet."

"Just one more question, Rabbi," Daniel said. "Can you give me the name of her closest friend in the congregation?"

"Rivka Aaronson," the rabbi said. He pulled out a pad of paper, scribbled the contact information on it, and handed it to Daniel.

Daniel accepted it as a dismissal, and he and Brenda rose to their feet and left the office, thanking the rabbi for his time.

"Pompous ass," said Brenda, once they had exited the shul and were walking toward their car.

"You think?" asked Daniel, with a grin.

"Sounds like a cult to me," she replied. "Can you imagine asking advice from him?"

"It does sound a bit like a cult, doesn't it? I had plenty of

Jewish friends in college. I can't recall that any of them had any trouble making their own decisions."

"Maybe some people find it easier when life is tightly proscribed. This isn't the only religious group like this. I grew up with a mother who was a born-again Evangelical Christian. Couldn't get away fast enough," Brenda said.

"So, you have some insight I lack," Daniel said. "Good to know."

"Did you really expect the rabbi to tell you anything useful? Even if he knew one of his married congregants had the hots for Beth, or hated her because she wasn't interested, he's not going to mention it. To hear him tell it, his congregation's only composed of the virtuous and the obedient. I don't suppose he could have been the boyfriend?"

Daniel sighed. "If he was, he was taking a big risk. If someone found out, he'd have been out of a job. On the other hand, sexual scandal is not unknown among religious leaders. A pregnant mistress is certainly a motive for murder."

"You didn't ask him for an alibi," Brenda said.

"Not yet. I want to find out more about the congregation, first," Daniel said.

"What's next, boss?"

"Why don't you take the lead when we interview Rivka Aaronson. She might respond better to another woman. We'll also interview Beth's friend, Jill. I promised Hannah Kline I'd meet her at Beth's apartment Friday morning. I'm sure she's never been to a murder scene before, and unfortunately, she got stuck with the job of packing up."

"Poor thing," Brenda said. "I don't envy her."

CHAPTER TWENTY-THREE

I GOT THROUGH MY OFFICE WEEK ON AUTOPILOT. I could manage pap smears and annual exams with my eyes closed, but it was harder when someone had abnormal bleeding or pain. Then, I actually had to think, and my brain was running on empty. It's hard to work out a differential diagnosis, plan all your imaging and blood tests, and think far enough ahead to decide what to do, depending on the myriad possible test results. It's a good thing I had a sympathetic staff.

My nurse followed me around with my prescription pad and radiology order sheets, gently reminding me not to forget things. My secretary screened my calls and only bothered me when it was essential. They conspired to keep my coffee cup full and to make sure I didn't skip lunch. I was going to have to give them all a giant Christmas bonus.

Friday morning, my stomach was in a knot. I didn't want to be the first to arrive, so I stopped at a Jiffy Doughnut place for breakfast. Daniel was waiting in front of the apartment when I got there at 10:15 a.m. He removed the yellow tape from the door and got out the keys. I was holding my breath as he opened the door.

The living room was much as I remembered it. An old gray sofa and two chairs, upholstered in cat hair, occupied one corner. Dusty stereo components filled one of the chairs, and an old-fashioned piano stood along the opposite wall. The dining table was covered with cartons and paperwork. The newly-painted white walls were dingy with fingerprint powder.

I gritted my teeth and followed him into the kitchen. Its bright yellow walls and the back door were covered in charcoal. The tray of wheat-free, sugar-free peanut butter cookies lay where I remembered them, minus the two Zoe and I had eaten. I didn't look to see whether any of the carving knives were missing.

Beth's study, with its wall-to-wall books and file cabinets, was the only room that looked orderly. Eventually I was going to have to go into the bedroom. The detective's look was sympathetic.

"I have to see it," I told him. "I've got to pack it all up."

Ross opened the door.

I reached for the support of the nearest wall.

The side table next to Beth's bed was knocked over. She must have fought. The twin size bed—Beth's statement that she had renounced her days of sexual liberation—was a mess, its flowered bed linens and quilt crumpled and dark with dried blood.

Blood had pooled on the floor and spattered the walls, which were streaked with fingerprint powder. Beth's dirty laundry, as usual, occupied every available surface.

The next thing I remember, Daniel Ross had an arm around my shoulders, and was helping me sit down on the living room couch.

"Stay here. I'm getting you a glass of water."

I heard him in the kitchen, heard the water running. Across the room, a brown plastic bag lay beside the piano. I got up and undid the tie. It was Beth's bear, the one that had sat in the white wicker rocking chair in her parent's house, a hundred years ago. Its arms and legs dangled by threads from its body. Zoe's bear. She had meant it for Zoe.

Ross came out of the kitchen with a glass in hand.

"It was supposed to be for Zoe." I started to cry.

Daniel Ross was a prince. He could have just sat there, handed me a handkerchief, and made sympathetic noises. Instead, he did the one thing that actually made a difference. He cleaned up. He threw out all the linens, took the mattress out to the dumpster, and put a clean sheet over the floor. When he was finished, all you could see were the dried drops on the wall, and I would have to live with that.

"I owe you one," I said to him. "I didn't realize how hard this was going to be."

"I did," he said. "You think you'll be able to handle it, but you never can, when it hits home."

I was only beginning to understand how right he was.

CHAPTER TWENTY-FOUR

AFTER DETECTIVE ROSS HAD FINISHED THE CLEANUP, I wanted to leave. I couldn't face being alone here. Tomorrow, at least, I'd have help.

"How about some lunch?" he asked.

I looked at him, noticing that he too, looked worn out. "I'd love some, thanks, detective, but it's my treat. What you just did for me was above and beyond the call of duty."

He smiled. "If you're going to treat me to lunch, you should call me Daniel."

I reciprocated with "Hannah," and steered him toward a soup-and-salad place that Beth had always liked. I even knew exactly what she would put on her salad. *Oh God, Beth, who would ever have thought, when you moved here, with such hopes and aspirations, that it would end like this?*

I made myself a large pile of disgustingly healthy-looking salad vegetables and topped it off with some diet dressing. Daniel, I noticed, had gone for chili with all the trimmings, and added a giant helping of pizza bread. This was one of the times when I truly hated men.

We spotted an empty booth, deposited our trays, and sat down with a mutual sigh of relief.

"I'm sorry I was such a basket case. It's not my usual style."

"I'm sure." he said. "I bet you're pretty impressive in an operating room."

I shook my head. "I don't feel impressive right now. I can barely manage to hold it together well enough to put one foot in front of the next. I'm dreading the weekend. I'll have to start going through all her things."

"I know," he said. "Do you have any help?"

I nodded. "My best friend, and hers."

"What about her immediate family?"

"They're all on the East Coast."

Daniel gave me a sympathetic look. "I can't remember a murder case I've handled that's felt so close to home. I live in the neighborhood, one of those little pedestrian streets just off the beach. It could have been my wife, or one of my neighbors."

So, he did have a wife. "Is your wife frightened because of this?" I asked.

Daniel shook his head. "Annie and I are divorced. She couldn't handle being married to a cop. It wasn't what she'd signed on for. I offered her the house, but she didn't want to live alone in that neighborhood. I guess she was right."

"I'm sorry," I said.

Actually, I wasn't. For some reason, I was pleased to hear he was divorced. I suppose it made me feel less of a fool for finding him attractive. It was absurd and annoying to be having a chemical reaction to a good-looking man, under these circumstances. I was probably just feeling vulnerable.

"Have you been divorced long?" I asked.

"About a year. Annie married me when I was a first-year law student at Stanford. I was supposed to finish law school, move to San Francisco, join my father's law firm, and father three children. It didn't work out that way."

"What happened?"

Daniel didn't look offended at my nosy question. "I hated law school. I quit after the first year, and then, for lack of anything better to do, I joined the military. Fortunately, we weren't in the middle of any wars at the time, and I got lots of good training without ever being in danger. When I got back, I decided to go to the police academy. I already knew all I needed to know about weapons. Maybe I had the illusion I could do something decent with those skills."

"Annie hated all of it," he continued. "She'd planned on marrying a successful lawyer, not a guy who came home with blood on his clothes at three in the morning. Maybe, if we'd been able to have those three children, it might have been different. But that didn't work out either. She never got pregnant, and the doctors were never able to figure out why. She finally decided to bail. I can't say I blame her. I don't suppose being married to me was a whole lot of fun."

"I understand the part about coming home at three in the morning, covered in blood. I do that frequently. My husband, Ben, used to refer to it as my *occupational hazard*."

He grinned at me.

I wanted to reach over and squeeze his hand, but I restrained myself. I was out of practice. I'd never been the sort to make the first move.

"What about you?" he asked. "How did you wind up in Los Angeles?"

"Ben, Beth's brother, was an architect. He specialized in historic renovations. After all those years at Harvard, in

Boston, we wanted to be someplace warm. He got a great job offer in LA, from a firm that did exactly what he loved, and I applied for every *Obstetrics and Gynecology* residency in Southern California. I was lucky enough to match at the County. After my residency, I started a practice at Memorial and I've been there ever since. Zoe was born there. Unfortunately, Ben didn't live to see her. He died a few months before she was born."

"I'm sorry," he said. "It must have been difficult for you, raising Zoe by yourself and running a practice. Have you told her what happened to Beth?"

"Only that her aunt died. Hardest thing I ever did."

Daniel reached over the table and put one of his large hands over mine.

The hand felt warm and comforting.

"I'm working all weekend, Hannah. Would it be okay if I stop by Beth's place, when I can, to make sure you're okay?"

"Private security service?" I asked.

He shook his head. "Just a buddy checking in. I like it better that way."

I put my other hand over his and squeezed, briefly. I liked it better that way too.

"Can I ask a buddy a few questions?" I asked.

"Sure," Daniel said. "And when you're done, I have a few for you too."

"Do you have any idea of who might have done this? Does the forensic evidence show anything?"

Daniel seemed to hesitate.

He probably wasn't allowed to talk about an ongoing investigation, but there was no harm in asking.

Finally, he nodded. "I can't tell you much, because we still don't know much. There were no fingerprints on the murder weapon or the doorknob, so either he wore gloves or he wiped the handle. We did get some material from under her nails. She tried to defend herself, so if we get a suspect, there's DNA we can match."

"What about her ex-husband?" I asked. "Are you going to get his DNA?"

"Josh Meyer seems to have an airtight alibi for the hours in question."

"Really?" I asked. "Is she half his age?"

Daniel raised an eyebrow. "Younger than that."

"I'm not surprised. What did you want to ask me?"

"Two things, actually." He reached into his pocket and pulled out a piece of paper, which he unfolded and handed to me. "This is a police artist's sketch of a man who made a pass at Beth in a restaurant, the night of her death. It's the witness's best recollection. Have you ever seen him before?"

I stared at the sketch. There was something familiar about it, but I couldn't put my finger on it. It nagged at me. "Do you mind if I keep this? It rings a bell, but I can't place it yet. Maybe, if I stare at it for a while, it will come back to me."

"Sure. We made lots of copies. One more thing, Hannah, and this is confidential, but I think you might be the best person to help me find this information. Beth's autopsy is complete. I know you told me she didn't have a boyfriend, but she was six weeks pregnant. Did you know?"

"Pregnant?! Are you sure?"

"Positive."

My jaw dropped. I couldn't believe it. Beth had always had lots of lovers, but she was very careful about birth control and protecting herself from sexually-transmitted diseases. I was in a position to know. I was her gynecologist. I could believe she hadn't told me about a recent sexual encounter, but to be careless enough to get pregnant... It made no sense.

"Beth told me she hadn't dated since the divorce, and I had no reason to doubt her. She did mention that she had recently become attracted to a client, but she assured me that he hadn't even asked her out yet."

"Do you know his name? "

I shook my head. "She didn't mention a name. I'm still astonished that she didn't tell me about this. I was her doctor. She was going to need either an obstetrician or an abortion. Either way, she would have turned to me."

"Perhaps she didn't know she was pregnant yet," Daniel suggested.

"Maybe. One of the things I'm hoping to do tomorrow is go through her files, so that I can return projects to the people she worked with. Why don't I make a list of all her clients for you?"

"I'd appreciate that," Daniel said. "We have our IT guy working on her computer. I'm assuming all the contact information for her clients is on it, but it certainly won't hurt to double check."

"Okay. I'll call you when I have it," I said. I did have one or two other ideas about Beth's pregnancy, but I wasn't going to mention them until I'd checked them out myself.

CHAPTER TWENTY-FIVE

S ATURDAY MORNING CAME TOO SOON. I DROPPED ZOE off at a friend's house for a play date, loaded my car with cardboard boxes, stopped by the supermarket for a supply of huge plastic garbage bags, and headed for Beth's. Lisa and I had agreed to meet there at ten, but neither of us was anxious to be the first one there. I spotted Lisa's Volvo parked across the street, and I honked as I pulled into a parking space in front of the building.

Lisa locked her car door and headed across the street to help me.

"Have you been waiting long?" I asked, as I started to unload.

"Five minutes or so," she said. "I left you the closer space."

I smiled at her, my arms full of boxes, and started carrying them toward the front door. Lisa grabbed a few from the trunk and followed me. I reached into my purse for the key, changed my mind, and headed back to the car for more boxes. We unloaded it completely, locked all the car doors and windows, and piled the cartons against the wall of the building.

Finally, we ran out of excuses.

I located the key and fumbled, turning it in the lock. The front door opened, and I stepped aside to allow Lisa into the apartment. A wave of depression came over me as I walked inside, but it was slightly less horrible than the first time.

"I've always hated this place," Lisa said. "I wanted her to move."

She ran a finger over the print powder and looked around at the bleak, cluttered living room. I moved the boxes inside and double-locked the door.

"Where did it happen?" she whispered. She looked pale and shaky in the dim light.

"In the bedroom," I said. "But it's cleaned up. It won't be as horrible as you think."

"I don't know if I can go in there, but I feel like I have to."

"I know, I felt that way too. We can start packing in here, if you prefer."

Lisa sat down on one of the dining room chairs. I'd met her any number of times, but I didn't really know her very well. I just knew that she was Beth's closest friend in LA, and probably knew more about Beth than I did.

"I think I'm ready now," she said, getting up.

I followed her into the bedroom and watched, as she took it in.

"Do you believe in premonition?" she asked.

I shrugged.

"The night she died, I was driving home about midnight. I'd been rehearsing with my band and suddenly, I was overcome with such a horrible sense of loss and sadness, I had to pull over. I couldn't stop crying, but I didn't have the slightest idea of what I was crying about."

She was crying now. I hugged her and we both cried together for a while.

Finally, I dug out some Kleenex. "What do you mean, you were rehearsing with your band?"

"Didn't I tell you, I'd started singing?" she asked. "It's great fun when you can do it as a hobby, and don't have to rely on it to make a living. I've got my first club date coming up in a week. Beth was going to come."

Vaguely, I recalled a notation I hadn't understood on Beth's calendar: *Lisa Sings.*

"That's terrific, Lisa," I said. "Can I come?"

"You'd better," she said. "I need the moral support. Well, where do we start?"

I looked around, debating. "I think it would be easiest to do the bedroom first. Most everything in it is going into the pile to be given away. We can stuff most of it in these giant bags, and once we're done, we don't have to go back in there, again."

Lisa nodded.

I started with the dresser drawers. Lacy camisoles, tiny bikini panties, delicate, see-through bras. I recognized a few things from her wedding shower. I imagined her wearing them under the long-sleeved, conservative clothes she had affected after becoming Orthodox.

One large drawer held exercise clothes, leotards in every color, matching tights, at least a dozen pair of leg warmers, several still in their original plastic wrap. I owned two leotards, both of which were falling apart. Clearly, Beth didn't believe in running out of anything. At the back of her exercise drawer, in a paper bag, were several black and red garter belts and black stockings. This was more than I wanted to know about Beth's sex life, and not a giveaway item for the Jewish Federation. I stuffed them into a garbage bag without commenting to Lisa. What else didn't I know about Beth?

"Look," said Lisa. "Her thrift shop finds. Beth would never have thrown these out." She held aloft a large feather boa, and a 1920s raccoon coat with a badly shredded lining.

Despite myself, I laughed. Beth's thrift shop finds were her pride and joy. Nothing made her happier than an Anne Klein silk blouse for two dollars and fifty cents.

Lisa started on the overstuffed closet, while I picked my way through a large pile of undone ironing.

"I'm sorting this into giveaways and good clothes," Lisa said. "She had some lovely things. Perhaps some of her friends would like to take them."

I was grateful Beth was three sizes smaller than I. I couldn't bear the thought of wearing her clothes, but I couldn't stand seeing everything she'd loved being given away to people she didn't even know. I walked over to the closet and thumbed through the things Lisa had saved. An olive-green suit brought a lump to my throat.

"Lisa, will you do something for me? Please take this home. I bought it for Beth on her last birthday, and I can't stand to see it become a thrift store item. In fact, you should take more of her nice clothes. I know she'd want you to have them. You're even the same size."

"I don't know if I could wear them," she said. "I'm afraid it would make me too sad."

"Maybe not now, but in a year or so, perhaps you'll feel differently. It might make you feel closer to her," I said.

"Okay, I'll take some home."

"I don't know if I'm ever going to be able to make sense of what happened, or let go of it," I said.

"I know," Lisa said. "I can't either. But somehow, I think that if Beth could comment on what happened to her, she would be able to put it into context in some way, even though we can't. Beth believed that when bad things happened, either you needed them to happen in order to move on to the next place in your life, or that somehow you drew the bad things to you."

"But there is no next place in her life. And you can't possibly believe she deliberately courted death by leaving the damn door open."

"You don't know that there isn't a next place," Lisa said. "Beth believed in the afterlife, reincarnation, astral travel. In fact, she believed that she'd had astral experiences while she slept. We once promised one another that whoever died first would try to prove to the other person that there is an afterlife. I keep having fantasies that she's going to try and contact me."

"Let me know if you hear from her," I said.

CHAPTER TWENTY-SIX

NEXT, WE TACKLED THE BATHROOM. MOST OF THAT went into the garbage pile. Beth had everything in dozens—every brand of shampoo, conditioner, toothpaste, mouthwash and deodorant known to man—each opened and only partly used. Every prescription medication bottle she'd ever filled, since 1990, was in the drawer—some with one or two pills left, some empty.

I found a few expensive pieces of jewelry lying in a drawer: her pearls, her good watch, and a sapphire ring Evelyn had given her. I retrieved them for her parents.

By lunchtime, Lisa and I were both exhausted. I didn't have any appetite, but I needed to sit down for a while. Lisa had to leave, to finish the papers for a deal closing on Monday. Fortunately, I was expecting Andrea to arrive any minute.

Lisa waved to me as she got into her car. I hadn't realized what a nice woman she was. Maybe I'd get a babysitter for next weekend, drag my butt out of the house for a change, and go hear her sing.

Andrea drove up, just as Lisa was leaving, and I was relieved to see her. Being alone in Beth's apartment, even for a few minutes, was creeping me out.

Even in sweats and no make-up, Andrea looked stunning. She had the kind of long, thick, honey-blonde hair you only see in ads for Lady Clairol. If there truly was reincarnation, I was planning to be reborn with it.

"How are you sweetheart?" she asked.

"If I were any more depressed, I'd make you start me in therapy." I said.

I desperately wanted to tell Andrea about Beth's pregnancy, and to see if she knew anything, but I'd promised to respect Daniel's confidence.

She squeezed my hand. "I wish I thought it would help. I've been dreading this. I couldn't sleep at all last night, just thinking about it."

"Are you sure you want to do this?" I was afraid for a minute, that she'd change her mind and beg off.

"I have to. Five years of my life is on Beth's computer. I need to retrieve all our book notes, and my reference books, and I need to see the apartment again. Maybe it will make it real to me."

The study was the only organized room in the apartment, and most of the books and papers needed to be sent back to Connecticut. Those were the only things the family wanted.

"Where's her computer?" Andrea asked, a tinge of panic in her voice.

"The police have it. Don't worry. Her back-ups are here. Let's find the ones for your book."

Andrea searched in the vicinity of the desktop, while I

scanned the bookshelves. I've always thought that people's books were the most accurate reflection of their minds. I grew up in a house full of books, with a mother who made a weekly pilgrimage to the Brooklyn Public Library. I'd always felt confused, in the homes of friends whose parents didn't have any.

Beth had at least as many books as I did, and it had always amazed me that I was never able to find anything to borrow. Our tastes were completely different. Several shelves were devoted to a large collection of Judaica. The religious collection shared shelf space with volumes on sex and erotica, ranging from such classics as Masters and Johnson, to things like *The Tantric Yoga Guide to a Better Sex Life*. Then there was the self-improvement section: *How to Stop Procrastinating and Start Living*, *The Working Girl's Guide to Getting Rich*, *Holistic Therapies for Your Depression*, *How to Make Yourself Irresistible to Men*. There was a large collection about writing, including titles like *Overcoming Writer's Block*, and *Writing from the Inner Self*. The rest of the collection was mostly philosophy, pop-psychology and Eastern religions.

I scavenged a few well-used children's books for Zoe, and started packing the rest of it into cartons.

I glanced over at Andrea. "You okay? Have you found everything?"

"I'm going to miss her so much," she said. "She was such a wonderful character. No matter what your problem was, she'd always have an answer. Unfortunately, it was always a fifth-world answer. She'd refer you to some doctor she'd met on a bus, who'd just immigrated from Tibet. Or, she'd relate the advice she'd just gotten from her spirit guide, on her last astral trip. It was always so far from my world, that I'd sit there with my mouth open. I'd never traveled to where she had been."

"But you trusted her to edit your book, and you worked with her for five years. How come?"

Andrea smiled. It was a soft, nostalgic smile. "She was your sister-in-law. She was bright and warm, and funny, and had a good resume, and I didn't really want to write the damn book. She helped me procrastinate. The process of working on this thing was hell on wheels, but the ultimate outcome was terrific. I don't know if someone else could have done it differently, better or faster. I just know, I always felt her to be so loyal and supportive, and present for me, that I couldn't imagine working with anyone else. The truth is, I don't know if I'll ever be able to finish without her."

"You'd better," I said. "Can you imagine how pissed she'd be if you didn't?"

For someone who was as rotten a housekeeper as Beth, her files were remarkably well-organized. I scanned through the file drawers, before sealing each cabinet and labeling it with an address label for the movers. I was searching for the novels, hoping against hope that one or the other of her unfinished manuscripts was finished enough, that a skillful editor might be able to realize her dream for her. So far, I hadn't found them.

A file labeled *Eagle Articles* caught my eye, and what was in it made me catch my breath.

Beth's first job out of graduate school was as a fledgling reporter for the *Sunland Beach Eagle*, a local, now out-of-business, Orange County newspaper. The article I was staring at was written in 1993.

I've never understood how a man can rape a woman, and then go home and have dinner with his wife. How could a person murder someone or rob someone, and even go home at all? So, if one is going to be murdered, obviously there are murders and murders. If I had a choice about how I'd want to be murdered... Or, if I were going to be robbed, here are my demands...

"What did you find?" Andrea asked.

I passed it to her.

"God, this is eerie. It's like a voice from the grave, or a prophecy of doom. It's almost as if she predicted her own death, seventeen years ago."

"The rest of the article's all about robbery and rape," I said.

Andrea handed it back and I replaced it in the file folder.

"I think I found the novels," she said. "There seem to be a lot of manuscripts in this drawer."

I'd read the beginnings of both of Beth's novels before, so I recognized them immediately. She had a lot of hand-written notes on yellow paper, along with the neatly printed chapters. I found a small box and emptied the drawer's contents into it. I'd send them back to Irving and Evelyn, eventually, but I needed to reread them first myself. They felt like the only pieces of Beth that I could still hold on to.

"I've found something else," Andrea said. "You'd better come here and look."

CHAPTER TWENTY-SEVEN

Andrea was on the opposite side of the room, near a small bookcase.

"Beth's journals," Andrea said.

She handed me the volume she'd been looking at, and I leafed through it.

It was a cross between a writer's journal and a high school scrapbook—movie tickets, theatre programs, articles from the paper, letters from friends, photographs, pictures cut out of magazines—the memorabilia of her life stared up at me. Between the clippings, there were pages in Beth's hand. I couldn't bring myself to read them. It felt like the ultimate invasion of privacy.

"Are you going to destroy them?" Andrea asked.

"Destroy them?"

"She was such a private person," Andrea said. "Somehow, I can't believe she'd want her parents, or her brothers, to read what's in here."

I shook my head. I knew exactly what Andrea meant. I could think of a few things in my possession, I'd rather not have exposed to prying eyes. I vowed, then and there, to get rid of them. You never know when your time is up.

"I can't destroy them," I said. "It's not my place to do that. I can't begin to assume anything about what Beth would have wanted. Perhaps reading the journals will comfort her parents, and Beth would want them read for that reason." I closed the volume I'd been examining, and replaced it.

"I think it would be a big mistake to send them to her parents," Andrea said. "I think there are things you just don't want to know about your child."

"Why don't I box them, take them home, and let them sit for a while. Maybe this is the wrong time to make a decision about them."

"Good idea. Is there anything recent?" Andrea asked.

I scanned the shelf. The last large book was labeled 2009. Next to it was a slim volume, that looked like a child's composition book. It was almost empty. There were a few postcards from a Club Med. An obituary of Baghwan Shree Rajneesh, the guru with the eighty-five Rolls Royces. A concert program. A piece of yellow paper with a big sign written on it that said *Beth, Welcome Home* with a smiley face. An article about an Orthodox unemployed father of six, who'd won a five-million-dollar lottery.

An entry dated in March was a shopping list titled:

My Man

> *Feet on the ground.*
> *Ethical.*
> *Thinks ahead.*
> *Kind, generous.*
> *Thinks of me first. Thinks of us.*

Has his professional life together.
Sensual and sexual.
Can negotiate and compromise.
Even tempered, not high strung.
Appreciates my sense of humor.
Is someone whom I can really respect.

It was a great list. At this point in my life, I wouldn't mind being introduced to someone who met all those criteria either. What I could never understand was why, with such high standards, Beth had managed to be involved with so many creeps.

I turned the page and found the last journal entry. It was dated two months before her death and was only a short paragraph.

I've done it! I've committed myself irrevocably, and I'm thrilled and terrified at the same time. I decided not to ask the Rabbi. I'm afraid my decision is against Jewish law, and if it is, I don't want to know about it. I'm praying it works.

"What do you make of this?" I asked Andrea. "Do you know what she's talking about.

Andrea read the page and shook her head. "I have no idea, but she was behaving strangely in the weeks before she died."

"Strangely, how?"

"She was excited, agitated and she wouldn't tell me why. Instead, she pretended I was imagining it."

"I guess we'll never know what she meant," I said.

I closed the book and put it with her novels. It was just a small mystery, insignificant, beside the real question of why the universe had chosen Beth to die before her time.

Having Andrea with me was a huge help. She was truly a packing maven, and we finished the study much more quickly than I had imagined we would. There were still a few hours of light left, so we tackled the kitchen, throwing out all the open food, packing up some of Beth's nicer wedding presents for me to take home, and putting everything else in giveaway cartons.

"Don't throw this out," Andrea said, handing me a heavy bag full of tarnished flatware. "It's all sterling."

I noticed the .925 marking on the back of one of the spoons. A .925 marking meant the piece was sterling silver. An IS marking would have meant it was International Silver, but not necessarily sterling. I remembered that Beth used to collect sterling odds and ends from antique stores. My fingers were already black from touching it. It had obviously been a while since she'd entertained.

There was one more thing I needed to do, before we left the apartment. I had to check on Mittens. We went out on the back porch and knocked on the neighbor's door. A young skinny guy opened it.

"Hi," I said. "I'm Hannah Kline, Beth's sister-in- law. I'm cleaning out the apartment."

He smiled and held out a hand. "Frank Jeffreys."

"I figured. I haven't had a chance to thank you, for what you tried to do for Beth, or for taking care of the cat. I've been meaning to call."

"I only wish I'd had the nerve to go in there, before the police arrived."

"So he could have killed both of you? I heard the police were here within minutes, and it was still too late."

"How's Mittens doing?" Andrea asked.

"He's still hiding under the house," Frank said. "He's pretty spooked. He must have seen the whole thing. He's eating, though. I've been leaving food on the back porch for him. Have you found someone to take him yet?"

I shook my head. I hadn't even thought about it.

"What about you?" Andrea asked. "Don't you think Zoe would like him?"

No question. Zoe's only pets at present were two turtles, given to her on her last birthday by Emilia. She'd named them Leonardo and Donatello. The question was, would *I* like him?

I got down on my knees and peered under the crawl space.

Two red eyes reflected back at me.

"Come on, Mittens. Come on out. You don't have to be afraid. I'm family."

The eyes moved a little closer.

We stared at one other with mutual suspicion.

I held out a hand and he sniffed it. I withdrew, and grabbed a handful of Purina from the bowl on the back step.

He considered my offering. Finally, he licked it from my palm.

When he finished, I scratched the back of his ears, and was rewarded with a purr.

I sighed. It was the least I could do for Beth, and Zoe would be ecstatic.

Daniel stopped by just as Mittens and I were leaving.

"How are you doing?"

"Holding it together. Thanks for stopping by to check on me at the apartment. It's reassuring."

"I figured," he said. "Listen, tell me if you think I'm

being presumptuous, but I was wondering if you'd like to go out for a bite to eat, one night this week."

I hesitated. Zoe was pretty possessive of my evening time, and I rarely went out at night during the week, unless it was to Labor and Delivery.

"It's hard for me to get out during the week," I said. "But I was planning to hear Beth's friend Lisa perform next week, on Sunday night. She's singing at a club in West Hollywood. Would you like to come?"

Daniel smiled, with what seemed like genuine pleasure. "It sounds great. I think both of us could use a break."

CHAPTER TWENTY-EIGHT

I T DIDN'T TAKE DANIEL LONG TO IDENTIFY THE *JILL* ON the phone machine as Jill Phillips, and to arrange an interview. They met at her office, in a small building in Santa Monica. Jill was in her fifties, short and plump, with a sweet smile, and long, frizzy, gray hair. The sign on the office door said *Jill Phillips, Public Relations*.

Daniel got right to the point. "You may have been the last person to talk to Beth Kline before she died. I heard the messages you left on her phone. Did you talk to her on Sunday, about getting together?"

"Not on Sunday," Jill said. "We had spoken earlier in the week, but she sounded as if she was pretty swamped with work. Sunday night, she called and left a message at my house that she was having trouble concentrating, and would I like to go out and play for a while."

"Do you know what time she called?"

"I got home about 10:15 p.m., from an eight o'clock movie, so it must have been while I was gone. I called her right back, but there was no answer."

"Were you worried that she wasn't home at that hour?" Daniel asked.

"Not at all," Jill said. "Beth was a night person. She often stayed out late. I figured she had either found another friend to play with, or had gone out by herself. One of the things she liked about her apartment, was how close it was to nice stores and restaurants. If she felt like getting out, she could just walk to someplace that was lively."

"Was Beth the kind of woman who would pick up a guy at a bar or restaurant, and bring him home?" Daniel asked.

"I think she used to be," Jill said. "After she got divorced, she would entertain me with stories of guys she had dated before her marriage. Beth met men everywhere. Restaurants, bars, spiritual seminars, classes, the gym, her office, the bus, the beach. She was very open and probably too trusting. Then, she became Orthodox and really changed. I think her idea of how to meet the next man in her life was through an introduction from her rabbi. She didn't date at all, after she and Josh split up. She was really shaken by how badly she had misjudged his character, and didn't trust herself to get involved with anyone new."

"Thank you, Ms. Phillips. I appreciate your input," Daniel said.

Once again, Daniel thought about C.J.'s. Beth had certainly engaged in a conversation with Sam. Had he lied to them and gone home with her? Or had the guy in the sketch stalked her? He needed to do a more thorough job on Sam's alibi.

Brenda phoned Rivka Aaronson and asked if she and Daniel could come and talk to her about Beth. "The rabbi told us you were her closest friend in the congregation."

Rivka agreed and asked them to come at seven in the evening, after her six children had gone to bed. The Aaronsons lived in an enclave of brand new, expensive homes, not far from the Shul. She answered the doorbell and ushered Daniel and Brenda in with a smile. A small woman about Beth's age, she was casually dressed and wearing a headscarf. The house was immaculate and remarkably quiet.

"Don't tell me you managed to get six kids to bed before we got here?" Brenda asked.

"Oh, yes. I'm very strict about that," she said.

Rivka offered them a cup of tea and motioned them toward the living room sofa.

"I still remember the very first Shabbat Beth spent at our home," Rivka said. "In this community, when you come to the Shul for the first time, you can't get away without a meal. You're always invited home to someone's table. Beth and Joshua came to us. I was so impressed with her openness and honesty. There was such a sweetness about her.

"When they decided to join the community, the Rabbi asked me to be her Pesach buddy, to teach her how to prepare her house properly for the Seder. Beth was like a sponge. All she wanted was to get the information, so now that she had taken on this new way of life, everything would be done correctly. She took it on with such a beautiful freshness and excitement. Our community is very close. We have one rabbi, who is the authority and who transmits what is to be decided. We go to him for problems and he deals with everything."

"Was Beth close to the rabbi?" Brenda asked. "Did she consult him often?"

"Very close," Rivka said. "Beth had an inquiring mind and she was always asking him questions, often difficult ones, about Jewish law."

"Do you have any idea if she consulted him the Sunday she died?" Daniel asked.

"I'm certain she didn't," Rivka said. "The rabbi had other things on his mind that day. His wife had just given birth to their eighth child, and he was with her at the hospital. Members of the congregation volunteered to take care of his other children overnight, so he could stay with his wife."

So much for the rabbi as a suspect, Daniel thought. That's an easy enough alibi to check.

"Did you spend much time with Beth, after her divorce?" Brenda asked.

Rivka nodded. "I still remember the day she told me about the divorce. The first thing I asked was *who's leaving*? I was trembling at the time and thinking *please let him be the one to leave*. When she said she was staying, I put my arms around her and said 'We'll take good care of you. This is your place. You belong here.' It was actually after her divorce that we became really close. I saw her blossom to such a degree. It was remarkable to see how outgoing she became."

"Did Beth want to remarry?" Brenda asked. "Was she seeing anyone in the congregation?"

"I think she wanted to remarry once she found the right person, but she was taking her time. She wasn't ready to date, and as far as I know, she wasn't interested in anyone in the congregation. Almost all of our men are married. We would have had to cast a wider net to find her a suitable husband."

"By *we*, you mean..." Brenda asked.

"The community. We try to take care of our own. We would have tried to find her a match, when she was ready."

"Do you know of any men in the congregation who might have been interested in her?" Daniel asked.

Rivka shook her head. "As I said, detective, most of our men are married."

"Were you with her that last night?" Brenda asked. "Was anyone in the community, that you know of? She was out until past midnight and no one seems to know where she was."

Rivka shook her head. "I would have known if anyone saw her that night. The last time we saw her was Saturday, at lunch."

These were nice people, Daniel thought, as he and Brenda returned to their car. He could see how much they'd loved Beth and why she'd loved them. It was possible that, being a tight-knit group, the last thing they would do was share gossip with the police. But so far, everyone they'd interviewed had denied the idea that Beth had a lover. This suggested that she had been extremely discreet. Perhaps she had become involved with a married member of the congregation?

The only thing they had learned tonight had been the Sunday night whereabouts of the rabbi. They were certainly no closer to identifying the father of Beth's child. Daniel wondered how much longer it would be until the DNA results were back from the lab.

CHAPTER TWENTY-NINE

A s I sat on the sofa that evening, trying to concentrate on reading a novel, my thoughts kept going back to what I knew of Beth's life. Beth had spent her late 20s in a series of unsatisfactory romantic relationships, including a short-lived engagement to a con-man, who had cheated her out of a good deal of money.

After the fiasco with the crook, Beth had embarked upon her feminist phase. I'd discovered feminism in the early nineties, or to be more accurate, had it thrust upon me, courtesy of Harvard Med. Beth was a late convert, but a welcome one. As with all her enthusiasms, she embraced feminism wholeheartedly. She read the books, attended the meetings, stopped wearing makeup, traded her contact lenses in for wire rimmed glasses, and chopped her long auburn hair into a short, geometric cut that was extraordinarily unflattering.

In addition to her full-time editing job, she took on several freelance jobs for extra money. The ex-fiancée had run up quite a credit card bill.

"I need to learn to do without men," Beth had said. "I have to reach a place where I like myself enough to be happy, regardless of whether I get married. I've always relied on men to make me feel valued. I felt inadequate if I didn't have one around. It's time for me to figure out how to make myself feel valuable."

I applauded the sentiment at the time, and I continue to agree with it today. I only wished Beth had been able to live up to it.

It took Beth almost two years to get her credit cards under control. I was proud of her. She acquired a large number of new friends, started a small literary magazine, built up her freelance clientele, discovered photography, and began work on her first novel. It was a productive time and, near as I could tell, she seemed to be happy.

Looking back though, I wondered.

Lisa had a very different take on that period of Beth's life. "She was a great actress and a chronically depressed person," Lisa had told me. "She spent more time lying in bed, for days on end, than you and I will ever know about. She also tried every antidepressant known to man. When she got like that, she'd disappear from sight. She always presented herself as this wonderful, sweet person and she expended a tremendous amount of effort helping other people. But the truth was that she was angry, and she was never able to deal with her own anger."

"Angry about what?" I asked.

Lisa shook her head. "I sensed there was something but she would never talk about it. Maybe she thought people would see her as a bad person, if she got angry."

I didn't have a clue. I had mostly seen her when she was enthusiastic and happy. I remembered the excited phone call I'd received from her when, after a two-year hiatus, there was finally a new man in her life.

"I just met this wonderful man. This could be it, Hannah."

"Slow down," I said.

Beth laughed. "I promise, I'll make him pay for all our dates in cash."

I relented. "Tell me about him."

"His name's Peter and he's a composer—a working composer! He does a lot of television. He's only ten years older than I am, and he's got a great house in the Hollywood Hills."

I was a little suspicious. "Has he been married before?"

"Everyone in Los Angeles has been married before," Beth said.

I laughed. "Great. Why do I think he might not be all that anxious to marry again?"

"I can't wait for you and Ben to meet him," she said.

———

At the top of my long list of errands was a call to Peter, my number one favorite of the men in Beth's life. Beth had taken some fabulous photos of him, and I thought he might like to have them. I also wondered if he and Beth might have gotten together, in bed, once or twice, for old time's sake.

Peter was delighted to hear from me, so delighted, in fact, that he insisted I come over for lunch. "I want you to meet Melanie, and my fabulous new daughter, Caitlin."

"Do you still live in the same house?" I asked.

"Sure do," he said. "Do you remember how to get here or do you need directions?"

I remembered. It had been over ten years, but Ben and I had spent a lot of time in that house.

I stopped by my favorite kids' store and picked up an adorable outfit for Caitlin. I liked it so much, I bought it in a size five for Zoe. Then I threw it, and all the photos, into my trunk.

CHAPTER THIRTY

THE WINDING ROAD OFF LAUREL CANYON LOOKED THE same as I remembered it. The house was unremarkable from the front, set into the hillside, with a gate at street level. I remembered the huge backyard with the pool, and the parties Peter and Beth had held there.

I rang the bell and Peter buzzed me in. As I walked up the stairs to the front door, I was greeted by two large dogs, who were, fortunately, wagging their tails. Peter opened the front door, met me halfway down the stairs, and hugged me. It felt good to see him again.

Without the yarmulke he'd been wearing at the memorial service, I noticed that his sandy hair had grayed and thinned, but he was still slim and wiry, and his narrow face seemed not to have aged. Peter, at fifty, seemed to me much the same as Peter at thirty-eight.

Peter ushered me into the dining room and offered me a drink.

I settled on boysenberry juice, for lack of Diet Coke.

"Unfortunately, Melanie and Caitlin had a *Mommy and*

Me this afternoon, so they aren't here, but Melanie fixed us some tuna salad."

For a while, we talked about babies and work, and nibbled on tuna fish, but I knew why I had really come. I needed to talk about Beth. I wanted to know why this relationship, in which she'd been happier than I'd ever known her, had failed. I also wanted to find out if Peter was responsible for her pregnancy.

"I brought you a few things from Beth's apartment," I said. "I thought you'd like to have them."

I handed him the shopping bag and watched as he looked at the photos she'd taken, and the little book she'd written for him on his birthday. I thought I detected a faint trembling in his mouth, as he thanked me.

"You know," I said, "I don't think I ever knew how you and Beth met."

He smiled. "I was visiting my friend Jon's office. There was this incredible woman working for him as a temporary secretary, and she was tall and sexy, and I was completely taken by her. There was something about her sense of humor that kicked off my sense of humor. Did she ever tell you about our first date?"

I shook my head. She may have, but I couldn't remember.

"I used to be a champion race car driver," he said. "By the time I'd met Beth, I'd given it up, but I still had my racing stuff around. I drove over to pick her up, dressed in a complete fireproof driver's suit, with a crash helmet and goggles. She took one look at me, and practically fell on the floor laughing. Then, there was the first time she came over here. Beth was a dichotomy. In many ways, she was very traditional, yet she was also a nudist. She belonged to a nudist camp in Topanga Canyon. Anyway, here we were at the house, and we weren't even lovers yet. I'd gone to the bathroom to get something, and she just walked in without any clothes on and asked if she could take a shower. I was completely blown away."

I imagined, by the time he'd recovered his composure, they'd become lovers, but I was being tactful so I didn't ask.

"Beth was always looking for answers," he continued. "We went to the same meditation class."

I nodded, encouragingly. I was glad he seemed to want to talk about her.

"There was also a very militant side to her. Beth was very adamant about women's rights and about the fact that women had been treated as second-class citizens for a long time. I think, sometimes, in her dedication to those principles, she tended to confuse *me* with *them*. I think that was one of the reasons our relationship failed, because all I feel for her is love. Looking back, I tried to ask myself, why was it that we weren't together anymore? Was it my fault she married Josh? And then wound up getting murdered? If we had stayed together, none of that would have happened."

"Don't do that to yourself, Peter," I said. "Was it my fault, because I forgot to remind her to lock her back door, the day she died?"

He shook his head. "I asked myself why, with all of her sweetness and caring, didn't it work? She loved me very much, and I loved her, but there was a part of her that needed to go out and fight that battle. She included me in the list of the enemy, but I wasn't the enemy. There was so much anger."

I remembered the anger. I felt a flush of sympathy for Peter. I'd never thought about what it must feel like, to be at the other end of all that rage. "How long did it take for you and Beth to fall in love after you met?"

"About ten minutes. We just knew that there was something hot going on, and we went for one another. I hadn't lived with anybody for a long time. I'd been married and divorced, and I felt shy. I don't let people into my life easily. At first, Beth didn't want to move in and give up her apartment. I was ready before she was. We negotiated for a while, but we were lovers right away, and we were on the phone constantly. Finally, she moved in here."

Peter got up and fixed us both a cup of herbal tea, while I thought about what else I wanted to know. I felt obsessed by a need to discover Beth, to know her more deeply than I ever had in life.

"What was it like living with her?" I asked.

Peter laughed. "What I remember, first of all, was that when I met her, she was basically living in her Volkswagen. This car was her purse. It contained every paper she had ever had, every wrapper of every hamburger she had ever eaten, every bit of extra ketchup, the manuscripts she was working on. Her car was her briefcase, and I thought to myself, *holy shit, can I live with a person like this*? But her mind was very orderly, even though her automobile wasn't, so we did fine.

"We were both gregarious. Beth loved having people around. She and I shared the ability to find whatever glimmer of good there was in a person, and we both picked up strays a lot. She was probably the first woman I'd ever been with who was an intellectual. I'm a bright person but I wasn't well-educated or well-read. Most of my intelligence had been directed toward music. Beth opened up this amazing world to me of literature and plays."

"Was she working, while you were living together?" I asked.

Peter wrinkled his brows, trying to remember. "I don't

think so. I think she was trying to write. She was so witty, with that New York sense of humor. She used to say that when you died, you got two things when you went to heaven. A tape recording of everything you ever said while you were on hold, and the pair to all the socks you lost."

"Why do you think she was never successful as a writer?" I asked.

"Success is such an elusive thing. She was never lauded for her work, yet in the industry, she was considered a very successful editor. I thought she was destined for big things, but perhaps she was afraid of it."

I sighed, thinking for the thousandth time of what might have been. "I know you two managed to stay friends, even after you broke up."

He nodded. "We talked on the phone a lot. I always had a tender spot for her. I never met her husband. She called me after she met him, and said she was going to move down to Venice and live by the shul. She told me how happy she was, that she'd found a way to get close to God, the way she wanted to get close to God. It was her personal way to express her devotion, and to be who she was. I called her after she got married, but she felt that Josh might not like it, so I stopped. I didn't want to jeopardize her situation."

"Did you ever see her again?"

Peter shook his head. "She called me once, after she broke up with Josh. I was single too, and a part of me said, maybe we should get back together. But I was dating my wife then, so we never did. I remember though, there was a pull."

"I know," I said. "She felt it too. She told me about talking to you."

For a moment, I saw a tear hovering.

"Thank you for telling me that," he said. "There will always be a question in my heart about why it didn't work out. Maybe, if I had been in a different place in my life, I could have gotten past all the storms. It's so hard to answer, because I'm a different man now, driven by different things —my love for my wife and my daughter. But up until I met Melanie, my love for Beth was the most significant of my life. There was always love for her and there always will be."

My eyes were tearing as I left Peter's house. It warmed me to hear him talk about his love for Beth, and I believed that he truly hadn't seen her in the past year. I had one more theory about her pregnancy, but today was Saturday, and I'd have to wait until Monday to check it out. In the meantime, perhaps I could actually relax a little, and look forward to my first actual date in years.

CHAPTER THIRTY-ONE

I SLEPT IN ON SUNDAY MORNING, TOOK A LONG HOT shower, and took Zoe to the park, until it was time for me to get ready for my date with Daniel. I couldn't believe it had already been a month since Beth's death.

Lisa's show took place at a small West Hollywood nightclub, called Star City.

"The show's at eight," she told me. "If you want to, you can get a bite to eat there."

I'd booked a teenage babysitter, recommended by one of my neighbors, and told Daniel to pick me up at six. I figured that way, we'd have plenty of time for a leisurely dinner. Daniel was on time, but the sitter showed up at seven. We decided we'd eat at Star City, after all.

I hadn't had more than half-a-dozen dates since Zoe was born, and none of them had come back for seconds. Dating seemed too complicated. All my friends kept warning me to make the guy take an AIDS test, before I kissed him goodnight.

Daniel was looking extremely sexy and not at all cop-like. He was wearing gray tweed slacks and a muted gray and black sweater. I caught a scent of aftershave.

"Sorry about the sitter," I said, as he helped me into his car. "We can still grab a bite at the club."

"No problem," he said. "I came for the company, not the food."

"I have a great idea," I said, as I fastened my seat belt. "Let's not talk about the murder tonight. I just want to enjoy Lisa's show."

We parked on a side street and looked for the club. It was a basement place with a bright neon sign, and almost empty at seven-thirty.

"I'm sorry," the hostess said. "We're not seating for another twenty minutes."

My hopes for a snack disappeared. There were four gorgeous guys at the bar, and it took me a second to realize they were a little too pretty, and much more interested in Daniel than in me.

"Are you sure this is the right place?" he whispered.

"Positive," I said, leading him outside.

My stomach was growling and I was starting to get cranky. We walked to Santa Monica Boulevard, hoping for fast food. We settled for a supermarket across the street, bought two sandwiches at the deli counter, and ate them on the bench at the bus stop. Then we went back to the club.

By that time, the guys had left the bar and the place was filling with a yuppie crowd. I spotted a few faces I'd seen at the memorial service, and a few folks I thought were probably lawyers from Lisa's firm. We got a small table, too close to the band, and ordered drinks.

The house lights dimmed, and the spotlight walked Lisa to the stage. She looked sensational—tight black pants, a loose, oversized black shirt, and a top hat. The pianist played a few bars from *Phantom of the Opera* and Lisa started to sing. The last note of the final song was somewhere way above high C. She held it for what felt like at least five minutes. The crowd went wild. She acknowledged their applause, looking radiant. Her colleagues were in the front row, clapping loudly, along with everyone else.

"Thank you, all," Lisa said. "But will you respect me in the morning?"

After that, she did some rock tunes, some show tunes and some sixties classics.

Then, she paused. "This song is for my dear friend Beth, who couldn't be here tonight."

The band started to play *I'll be Seeing You.*

As I heard the familiar lyrics and the haunting melody, tears began to flow down my cheeks. I couldn't help it. It was the perfect tribute to someone whose memory would always haunt me.

Lisa's eyes were full of tears too. I marveled that her amazing voice didn't falter. I was expecting her to break down any minute.

The song brought the house down. There wasn't a dry eye among those who knew what the song really meant, nor among those who had no idea. Daniel reached over and put an arm around my shoulders. I let it stay there, grateful for the comfort.

Lisa finished off with a few livelier numbers, and a standing ovation. I wondered what her law partners would have to say on Monday.

"She was great," Daniel said, as we walked back to the car.

"I'm glad you enjoyed it," I said. "Sorry about the dinner fiasco."

"Gives me a good excuse to ask you out again. Is it okay if I call? I know this is a rough time and I don't mean to rush you."

What a sweet man. I was surprised at the fact that I actually wanted to see him again. I fought an urge to caress his smoothly shaven face. "I appreciate having some company. I'd like you to call."

He delivered me to my front door, and left me with a kiss on the cheek.

For the first time in a month, I thought I might actually get a good night's sleep.

CHAPTER THIRTY-TWO

THE NEXT DAY, DANIEL SAT AT HIS DESK, THE CONTENTS of the Beth Kline file once again spread out in front of him. His professional detachment was deserting him, and he was feeling angry and frustrated. Apart from his professional irritation at not being further along, Daniel felt that he needed to solve this crime for Hannah, and that was yet another source of conflict and confusion.

He had never attempted to date a woman he'd met during a case, and the sensible part of him had looked on in disapproval, when he had asked her out. However, Daniel wasn't being ruled at that moment by *sensible*. He'd been powerfully attracted to Hannah, the moment they met. It wasn't just the fact that he found her beautiful and sexy. He was drawn to her intelligence, her warmth and vulnerability. He found himself wanting to take care of her, even more than he wanted to take her to bed, and he had wanted to do that last night, very badly.

Daniel was smart enough to recognize that any seduction moves would be a mistake right now. Hannah clearly wasn't looking for a serious relationship, and was too wounded to participate in one. He, however, was willing to be patient. Hannah was clearly a woman worth waiting for.

With a sigh, he opened his laptop, and started catching up on his reports.

CHAPTER THIRTY-THREE

HAVING ELIMINATED PETER, AT LEAST IN MY MIND, AS responsible for Beth's pregnancy, the first thing I did when I got to my office on Monday morning, was to pull Beth's chart. I'd functioned as her gynecologist, as well as her sister-in-law, for years—a job that had consisted of doing her annual pap smears and keeping her well-supplied with birth control pills. The last time I'd seen her professionally had been about a year after her marriage. She'd stopped using contraceptives and was concerned that she had not become pregnant. I'd asked her to come back for an estrogen evaluation on the second day of her next cycle, taught her how to identify the day of ovulation, and tactfully suggested that Josh have a sperm analysis.

She was quite certain he would be unwilling to do that, convinced that his twenty-five-year-old son was adequate proof of his virility. She had never followed up with any of my testing suggestions, and I hadn't reminded her. By that time, I had developed a thorough dislike of Josh, and was convinced that it would be a major mistake for her to have a child with him. When Daniel told me that Beth had been pregnant, I was blown away. I'd have been less shocked if he'd told me she was running a kosher house of prostitution.

On the other hand, someone had to have fathered that child. You only get to have an immaculate conception if you're utilizing the new reproductive technology. That was my next guess, but I wanted to confirm it, before suggesting it to Daniel.

Confirmation required only one phone call. Dr. Louise Waldman worked at the Beverly Hills Reproductive Institute. It was the largest and most respected infertility practice on the Westside, and the best bet for tracking down my answer. I'd met Louise right after I'd moved to LA. I'd liked her brisk, competent, professional manner, and had referred all my difficult infertility cases to her.

"Hannah, I just heard about your sister-in-law. I'm so sorry," she said.

"Thanks," I said. "I have something to ask you. Beth was my patient before her death."

"What do you need to know?"

"The autopsy revealed an early pregnancy. Could you check your computer and see if Beth was a patient at the Institute?"

"I don't need a computer to answer that. She was my patient and I particularly remember her because she was your sister-in-law. She was so bright and so funny."

"Did you know she was pregnant?"

"Of course, I knew. But Beth didn't," Louise said. "She suspected, of course. We ran a pregnancy test the Friday before she died, but the result didn't come back until Monday."

"Do you know who the father was?" I asked.

"Didn't Beth tell you? We were performing artificial

insemination for her, using a sperm bank donor. She got pregnant on the first try. She told me she wanted a child more than anything in the world, and that if Prince Charming refused to ride up on his white horse and father it for her, she was going to do it herself."

"I thought so," I said. "I just needed you to confirm it for me."

So, I'd guessed right. The pieces were beginning to fall into place. Beth must have been excited and agitated coming to this decision, and performing the act that finally committed her to it. The artificial insemination would explain her last journal entry. Andrea had noticed how hyper she'd been in the weeks preceding her death. She'd probably been uncertain of how her rabbi would interpret Jewish law on the subject, although she must have suspected artificial insemination would be frowned upon.

But, what had happened to make her so depressed afterwards? Had she decided she'd made an awful mistake? It still didn't make sense. Some of the pieces fit together, but half the puzzle was still missing.

Nevertheless, it was certainly time to share my information with Daniel. I reached for the phone.

CHAPTER THIRTY-FOUR

DANIEL THANKED HANNAH, AND HUNG UP. ON THE ONE hand, he was grateful to her for the information. He would have had much more difficulty probing the privacy of Beth's medical records, and artificial insemination hadn't crossed his mind. On the other hand, Hannah had just cut off his most promising avenue of investigation. Clearly, some anonymous sperm donor wouldn't have had much of a motive for murder.

He was at a loss for where to go next. But, as a courtesy, he should call Ian Scofield and cancel his request for a paternity cross-check between Beth's fetus and her killer. He picked up the phone and dialed.

"I was just about to call you," Ian said. "I've got your results. The paternity test was negative."

"I already know that," Daniel said. "I just found out she was doing artificial insemination at some infertility clinic."

"Now, that is interesting," Ian said. "It makes the rest of what I have to tell you even more important."

"What's that?" Daniel asked.

"Well, the fetus was male, so the first thing the lab did

was compare the Y chromosome with that of her killer. They would have been identical if he was the father, and they were quite different. The surprise was that there were a very large number of identical sequences in the remainder of the DNA. That means that the man who killed her was related to the fetus. Since you say the father was an anonymous donor, the odds are that Beth was killed by one of her relatives. I'd have to cross-check his DNA specimen with hers, but I'd start looking at close family— father, uncles, brothers, maybe first cousins. She have any family living in LA?"

"Just her widowed sister-in-law. One brother is dead. I don't know all the details of her extended family yet, but I'm about to find out. Thanks Ian. Just when I thought the gods of forensics had completely deserted me, you came through."

"Anytime," Ian said.

It took Daniel and Brenda an entire day of computer time to track down all the extended members of Beth Kline's family. He had considered asking Hannah for a quick rundown of the family tree, but decided against it. He didn't want her to know that he was looking at her extended family, and revealing the DNA findings of a case in progress was totally against the rules.

He was also beginning to worry about her safety. If Beth's killer had been a family member, it was possible that Hannah knew him. And the less she knew about the case, the less likely she would be to let something slip, that might get her killed.

Irving had been the youngest of five brothers. One was

deceased. Daniel had trouble imagining Beth being stabbed to death by one of her eighty-year-old uncles. Beth had two living, younger twin brothers, Jeremy and Jared. There were no male maternal first cousins, but quite a few on the paternal side. Most of them lived in Israel, but there were two on the East Coast.

"I say we check out the brothers first," Brenda said. "They were obviously the closest to her and I can think of a motive. Irving's pretty wealthy. With Beth and the oldest brother dead, they would get to split all the money."

"Maybe," Daniel said. "Let's see if either of them has a record, and let's check out flights from Hartford to LA within a week of the murder. To kill her, one of them would have to have been here. Let's do the same for the two East Coast cousins, and see what that gets us."

CHAPTER THIRTY-FIVE

INISHING BETH'S APARTMENT WAS A HUGE RELIEF. Mittens settled into living in Brentwood as if he'd been born there. Zoe spent half her time hugging him, and the other half inventing creative cat toys. Emilia fed him fresh tuna, scraps of sirloin steak and low-fat milk. I looked a bit askance at the cat food budget, but at least it kept him from going after Leonardo and Donatello.

I did my best to keep in touch with Ben's parents. Every few days, I called Irving and Evelyn, and tried to sound cheerful. Evelyn was doing poorly. She'd lost weight, didn't want to see anyone, and had managed to fracture her hip in a fall on the stairs. Irving was holding it all together by going through Beth's unpaid bills, and setting up scholarship funds in her name.

"She had almost a hundred charge cards," he told me, incredulously. "And she used them all! I always told her, Beth, you need to be more responsible about money. I was always bailing her out."

He sounded extraordinarily annoyed that she'd left him this mess. I wondered if the few thousand dollars in her savings account would be enough to handle her debts. I'd already returned her new car to the dealer.

I finally decided to tackle the cartons I'd stuffed into my storage locker. There were souvenirs of Beth that I wanted to keep, items I wanted to give to her friends, and things I needed to sort through, before I threw them away. The first thing I took out was the bear.

Sewing happens to be one of my fortes. I reinforced the arms and legs with surgical suture, and I left him sitting, as a surprise, on Zoe's bed.

Her eyes were shining when she found him. "Thank you, Mommy, for my bear."

"You're welcome, sweetheart. He's a present from Aunt Beth. He was hers, when she was a little girl, and she wanted you to have him."

"Mommy, let's play." She dragged out another bear from her huge collection. "This is the Mommy Bear." Then, she pointed to her latest acquisition. "This is the Baby. The Mommy and the Baby go to sleep, and then the Mommy Bear dies and goes up in the sky. Then, the Baby sees a bear, far away, and she finds her, and it's her Mommy come back."

Seemed like a good game to me. I was beginning to understand why child psychiatrists liked play therapy. Kids really put it all out there. I'd have liked to see Beth come back from the sky myself, and I should have realized that her loss would trigger Zoe's anxieties about losing me, too. We play-acted it about a dozen times, before my patience ran out. I needed a new project, so I decided to enlist Zoe's help with the silver.

I'd brought home a heavy plastic bag full of filthy flatware. I felt this absurd need to polish it, as though I were cleaning up the remnants of Beth's life, literally and figuratively. I sprayed the stuff with silver polish and rubbed it clean, while Zoe washed it with detergent and dried. When we finished, we had matching silver plate for eight and sterling for twelve, although the sterling was in an assortment of thrift shop patterns. I was surprised at how lovely it was. Irving had already said he had no use for it, so I decided to buy a silver chest and keep it. It was the sort of memento that wouldn't stick a knife in my gut, every time I saw it.

The box containing Beth's unfinished novels sat on my desk. She'd started the first one the year she'd met Peter. It was about a woman CIA operative named Wanda Wasserstein, whose adventures were as unlikely as her name. Wanda was always good for a few laughs, and I'd awaited each chapter eagerly, as Beth had spewed them forth from her computer. Unfortunately, though Wanda had plenty of wit, she lacked a good plot line, and Beth had regretfully abandoned her, after a two-year struggle with writer's block.

I'd always believed that Beth had a bestseller inside of her. I'd read enough popular fiction on airplanes to recognize how witty, funny and imaginative she was. My fantasy had been to finish her last novel. I don't mean personally. I couldn't write my way out of a paper bag, on anything but a medical chart. What I had in mind, was to hire a writer or editor to take her synopsis and finish the last chapter or two, so that I could make her dream come true, even if was posthumously.

My illusions were shattered pretty quickly. She had a synopsis and a hundred and twenty pages—the same one hundred and twenty pages that I'd read before her wedding. There were some handwritten notes, researching the historical data for the second section, but nothing else. There just wasn't enough.

When I thought about Beth's death, the thing that broke me up the most, was how unfinished her life had been. The good marriage she'd never found. The children she'd wanted so desperately and never had. The unpaid bills, and the tantalizing fragments of manuscripts that could have been wonderful books.

I was brooding over it, when the phone rang.

"Hannah, it's Marsha Blinderman."

"Marsha! Are you still in Connecticut?" It had only been three weeks since the funeral, and I thought Marsha might have stayed to spend time with her parents.

"No," she said. "I'm calling from Tel Aviv, so I'll make it quick. I want to come out to LA."

"I'd love to see you," I said. "When?"

"Next weekend. I'm having a hard time. I thought it would help to see you, and meet some of her friends. Beth and I used to talk every week. I'm not used to having a phone bill under two hundred dollars a month."

I laughed. "You're welcome to stay with me, Marsha. In fact, I insist. Just let me know when your flight lands, so I can pick you up."

Marsha and I hugged each other for a long time at the airport. When we got back to my place, I helped her unpack in Zoe's room. Zoe had no objection to bunking with Mom, and was more than thrilled with the collection of presents Marsha had brought for her.

After I calmed Zoe down and put her to bed, I settled Marsha in the kitchen with a cup of tea and a cheese Danish.

"I've thought about you a lot over the past few weeks," I

said. "It must be harder for you than for anyone. I know of no one who was closer to Beth."

Marsha sighed. "We were ten years old when we met. I can't remember back much further than that. She was a part of my life, for all of my conscious memory."

"We used to double-date in the tenth and eleventh grades, and make out in the back seat of cars. I lost my virginity in high school. Beth was in college when it happened to her. She sent me this letter with no beginning and no end—just lots of quotes from Khalil Gibran and a message that said, *when the time is right for a woman, she does it.* I understood that I wasn't to tell a soul, because the guy she got involved with was a professor at her school, a lot older than she was and married. She was mad about him until the middle of her freshman year."

"What happened then?"

"He dropped her," Marsha said. "Son of a bitch. His wife probably found out."

"I never heard that story," I said. "She must have been pretty upset."

"Devastated, but she got over it," Marsha said. "Beth loved sex. It was one of her great discoveries. She used to terrify me. She'd go out on first dates, sometimes blind ones, with her diaphragm in her purse. She felt she was just being honest about it. If boys could do it, why couldn't she?"

"Why do you think she only wanted to be with older men?" I asked. "I can't remember her ever looking at someone her own age."

Marsha got up, went to the stove, and poured more hot water into her mug. "All of her relationships with these older men were rather clandestine. It added to the excitement for her. She didn't care if they were married or not

Jewish. It didn't matter. I think she wanted a man who was already established, and who would take care of her and pay the bills—a patron of the arts. She had this vision of herself staying home, writing her novels, and sitting by the fireplace in a long skirt, with a cup of herbal tea."

"The more important question," Marsha went on, "was why the men she picked, up to and including her ex-husband, were so horrible. She seemed to ask of her relationships the punishments she couldn't mete out to herself."

"Punishments for what?" I asked.

Marsha shook her head. "Who knows? For not being the perfect daughter? For not living up to her own expectations of herself? She was sitting in her own private hell and hiding it from everyone."

CHAPTER THIRTY-SIX

T HE NEXT EVENING, I THREW A DINNER PARTY IN Marsha's honor. I hadn't entertained since Ben died. Emilia made a seafood risotto, green salad, and homemade apple crisp with ice cream. I invited Andrea and Lisa.

"You know," said Andrea. "Beth would not have approved of the menu."

Marsha speared a shrimp with gusto. "Am I the only one alive who can testify to the fact that Beth loved to eat link sausages?"

"I remember when she was on the *Korean Pork Diet*," I said. "As I recall, that was the one between the *Zucchini and Apple Diet* and the *Beverly Hills Diet*. I never could keep track of what her psychic nutritionist told her to eat."

"Beth," Marsha said, "was the world's greatest hypochondriac. She needed desperately to believe she was the victim of genetics, biochemistry, and strange mishaps in the body, involving no emotional elements. Her two chief ailments were migraines and constipation. She would wear special magic bracelets to ward off the migraines. She gave up wheat in the interest of doody-making. In the meantime, there were no big doodies made."

"I went nuts when she became kosher," I said. "For six years, she ate at my house, practically once a week. Then, all of a sudden, my kitchen was contaminated. She used to bring her own chicken and microwave it on a paper plate." I helped myself to seconds of the risotto.

"She always did everything to the *nth* degree," said Andrea. "It was who she was. Whatever she was into for the moment, she embraced completely. I was never able to figure out how she reconciled her feminism with the ultra-orthodox community she joined. She had to go to the Rabbi with her white squares of cloth, every month, after the Mikveh, so he could declare her clean. The rabbi, not even a woman attendant!"

"What white cloth?" asked Lisa.

Lisa was the only one at the table who'd been raised Catholic.

"You have to wipe yourself, an inch into the vagina after the ritual bath," Andrea explained. "Then you show the rabbi the cloth, to prove you aren't bleeding anymore. I think she was embarrassed about it."

Lisa made a face.

"I'd never met anyone as observant as she was," said Andrea. "It really used to bother me when she'd do things like refuse to take antibiotics for her bronchitis, because they weren't kosher."

"And this was a girl," Marsha said, "who screamed at me once in college, because I objected to some boyfriend of hers who wasn't Jewish. 'I'm sick of you,' she said. 'You live in a deep freeze with a Jewish star on it.'"

"Times change," Andrea said. "Did you and Beth ever live together?" she asked Marsha.

Marsha grinned. "The summer between our junior and senior years, we both had jobs in New York and we tried living together in Brooklyn Heights. We had a great time. Toward the end of the summer, I went out for a drink with a woman I was working with and she came on to me. I was really upset, and I came home to Beth and said, 'Beth, have I got it all wrong? Maybe I'm a lesbian.' 'Maybe you're Rumanian,' she said. 'I gotta find out,' I said. 'You're my best friend. You have to help me.' So, I start moving to kiss her and she backs off. 'What's wrong?' I asked. 'I don't know if you're a lesbian or not,' she said. 'But when you opened your mouth and pursed your lips, I knew I wasn't.'"

I started to laugh, and so did everyone else. It was a loud, hearty laugh. I could almost hear Beth deliver the punch line, and I realized I hadn't laughed that hard since she died. In some very small way, I felt I had turned a corner.

After dinner, we retired to the living room for coffee and Amaretto. I'd pulled a few things from those cartons that I thought her friends might want as keepsakes, and set them out on the buffet. I'd already given Marsha the collection of her letters, that Beth had saved since high school. I'd also pulled out a few selected photos and several boxes of costume jewelry.

Jill was rummaging in one of them, when she found a key. "I think this is a safe deposit key. Did Beth have a box?"

"I have no idea," I said. "I suppose she could have. That might account for the fact that I haven't found several pieces of her good jewelry."

"Where do you think it would be?" Andrea asked.

I shrugged. Beth had had at least four separate bank accounts. I'd have to start calling. I made a note on the bottom of my extensive list of errands.

Before I forgot, I pulled out the sketch Daniel had given me, and passed it around. "This is a police rendering of a man who apparently tried to pick Beth up in a restaurant, the night she died. There's something about him that looks vaguely familiar to me, but I haven't been able to place it. Does he look familiar to any of you?"

Marsha stared at the picture for a longer time than anyone else. Finally, she looked up with a puzzled expression on her face. "He reminds me of Ben," she said. "Look at the eyes and the facial shape."

I reexamined the sketch. The light eye color and the long hair had prevented me from seeing it, but Marsha was right. He bore a family resemblance to Beth and her brothers. It was a little eerie. I still had the sense that I'd seen him somewhere, but I couldn't remember. Maybe I was just imagining it, because the face itself seemed familiar. I wasn't sure if I wanted to tell Daniel.

CHAPTER THIRTY-SEVEN

THE MONDAY MORNING TEAM MEETING WAS WELL underway, when Daniel arrived. At least, everyone had poured their coffee, and helped themselves to doughnuts. Daniel wondered why everyone in the LAPD didn't experience early death from heart disease.

"Okay, everyone. Let's get started," he said. "Brenda has been checking on the males in Beth Kline's family."

Brenda turned on her computer and plugged in the LCD projector. She projected a family tree onto the white board at the front of the room. "It's remarkable how much information you can get off the web, without even consulting law enforcement databases. This is the Kline family tree. Someone posted it on Ancestry.com. Irving Kline had three sons. Ben, deceased as of six years ago, and younger, identical twin brothers, Jeremy and Jared, who are still living. Here are their Facebook photos. They're thirty-five years old, and they manage their father's insurance brokerage business. For comparison, here is the sketch of the suspect our bartender identified."

The twins had dark hair, closely cut, narrow faces, high

cheekbones and dark, slightly slanted eyes. Add a long wig, change the eye color, and there was a definite resemblance to the sketch.

"I checked passenger lists for all flights from Hartford and Providence going to Los Angeles within two weeks of the murder. No Klines," Brenda said. "However, Jared Kline did fly to Las Vegas, the Friday before Beth's murder, and flew home on Monday. Neither of the two East Coast cousins flew anywhere. Ditto for the Israelis."

"Do we know where Jared stayed in Las Vegas?" Daniel asked.

"He rented a car at the airport, and stayed at the Bellagio. LA is only a five-hour drive. I've contacted the LVPD, to see if they can get us security tapes from the hotel for the weekend, and to check on the mileage on the rental car."

"Good work," Daniel said. "How's the search going, for the guy in the sketch?"

Jose Mendez, one of the patrolmen on Daniel's team, stood up. "We're getting there," he said. "The manager of the Venice Community Homeless Shelter recognized the sketch. She said the guy's name is Randy, and he'd spent several nights there, over the past two months. Last time he was in, was two weeks ago."

"Here's what's next," Daniel said. "I've got a contact at Hartford PD. Someone needs to interview Jared Kline, and establish if he has an alibi or not. I want to make sure we aren't overlooking something. Jose, take two more guys and go back to that shelter in Venice. Interview every single person who's stayed there in recent weeks. See if you can find anyone else who remembers Randy. If he didn't sleep at the shelter, he had to sleep somewhere. Recheck the local homeless camps, and every motel in a two- mile radius. We need a last name, and we need to bring this guy in for questioning."

There was one more thing Daniel needed to do and he'd been hesitating. Hannah had said that the sketch looked familiar. He had avoided asking if it reminded her of anyone in her family.

He was going to have to speak to her

CHAPTER THIRTY-EIGHT

THERE WERE AN AMAZING NUMBER OF BANKS IN Santa Monica and West Los Angeles, and trying to find the time to make phone calls between patients was a challenge. Fortunately, I unearthed Beth's safety deposit box on the fifth phone call.

After work, I ran down to Chase bank. Armed with Beth's death certificate, the key, and a letter from her father granting me access, I was allowed to open the box.

There was a large pile of hundred-dollar bills lying on top. I counted them carefully, put them in an envelope, and placed it in my purse. A stash of four thousand dollars. No doubt it was her security blanket for leaving Josh. There were a few pieces of good jewelry: an antique locket, pearl earrings and a heavy silver bracelet. Finally, there was a collection of papers. I scanned them rapidly. Beth's birth certificate, marriage certificate and divorce papers, the deed to her car, and a white envelope.

The envelope contained a birth certificate, dated 1991, for a baby boy Kline, born in Ames, Iowa. There was a copy of a letter, dated six months ago, from Beth to an Iowa adoption agency. It stated that she had given birth twenty years ago to a male child, who had been given up for adoption. She would very much like to find him and make contact. All her contact information was provided. An answering letter told her that the agency had located her son, and had transmitted the request and the information. It would be up to him to decide if he wanted to meet his birth mother.

I sat there stunned, my mouth open and my hands shaking. I couldn't believe it. How could Beth have gotten away with giving birth, with none of her friends and family knowing about it? Marsha must have known. Why hadn't she told me?

I had to call her and then, I needed to tell Daniel. I didn't know if this information had any bearing on Beth's murder, but it wasn't something I could withhold.

CHAPTER THIRTY-NINE

I CHECKED MY WATCH AND ADDED TEN HOURS. MARSHA should be back in Tel Aviv and awake. I dialed her number.

"Hannah! How is everything in LA?"

"I'm hanging in there," I said. "I just made a discovery, and I need to ask you about it."

"Something about Beth?"

"Do you remember anything about the summer of 1991? Beth was in Iowa."

"Oh, yeah," Marsha said. "She got into some prestigious summer writer's workshop at the University. I didn't see her, till she came home in September. I wanted to visit her, but she was busy sulking over that married professor who'd left her flat."

"She didn't confide in you that summer?"

"About what?" Marsha asked.

"I found a birth certificate. She was pregnant when she went to Iowa. She had a child and gave him up for adoption. That's probably why she didn't want you to visit."

The silence lasted so long, I thought we'd been disconnected.

"Oh, God." Marsha's voice sounded as if she were crying. "I thought I was her best friend. I loved her and she didn't tell me. Don't you see what this means? She never really trusted me."

"Marsha, maybe it had nothing to do with you. Maybe it was just so painful, she couldn't talk about it to anyone."

"No, it was me she didn't trust," Marsha said. "She was afraid I couldn't keep my trap shut. I blew it over her letter. It was our first big fight."

"What letter?" I asked.

"She wrote to me about losing her virginity. I used to read her letters to my sister, because they were so funny. I started reading that one out loud, before I got to the part where she said not to tell anyone, under pain of death. I had to tell her what happened. She was furious with me. After that, she always put a code on the outside of the envelope if she was writing anything personal—FYEO—for your eyes only. It was our private joke."

"Maybe she felt the stakes were so high, the only way she could be sure of secrecy, was to not tell anyone. Her parents would have been furious."

"Are you going to tell them?" Marsha asked.

"No," I said. "There's something else. Beth wrote to the adoption agency just before she died, trying to find her son. They wrote back and said they couldn't give her any information, but they could try to contact him and give him the option to get in touch with her. There's no point in telling her parents, unless I can present them with a grandchild they didn't know they had. It would just be one more horrible loss. Beth spent her life hiding this from them, so she wouldn't hurt them. I don't see any reason now to change that."

I listened to Marsha cry for a while longer, then I hung up and rummaged through my closet for something to wear to the office. No point in hurrying. I didn't have patients scheduled until the afternoon, and I still needed to talk to Daniel.

CHAPTER FORTY

W HEN HANNAH CALLED, DANIEL WAS IN HIS CAR, ON his way to interview a witness in a recent gang shooting. Beth Kline's murder, although it was still in the forefront of his mind, didn't preclude his team having to work other murders, simultaneously. They'd been given a month to work the Kline case exclusively, and then the captain put them back on rotation. The need for multitasking was Daniel's greatest job frustration. Sometimes, he felt as if he were juggling so many plates at once, he'd never be able to prevent several of them from crashing to the floor.

He put the call on hands-free and greeted her. "I was about to call you. I have a couple questions."

"Daniel," she interrupted. "I need to see you. I've found something that may be important. Is there any chance we can meet, before I have to leave for my one o'clock office?"

"I'm in Santa Monica," he said. "Where are you?"

"At home. I could meet you anywhere in Santa Monica, if you aren't tied up with something."

"I'm not," he said. "How about the Peet's on Montana?"

"I'll be there in fifteen minutes," she said.

Hannah was as good as her word, and walked in looking gorgeous and professional at the same time. She was wearing a long taupe skirt with brown suede boots, and a soft green sweater that highlighted her eyes. He felt a surge of desire and wanted to greet her with an unprofessional hug, but he restrained himself, and settled for a smile and an offer of a latte.

They took their coffees outside to a table with some privacy.

Hannah reached into her purse for a white envelope. "I found this in her safe deposit box. I don't know if it has any bearing on her death, but I thought you should know."

Daniel took out the papers and read them carefully. "May I keep these? I can make copies for you, until I can return the originals."

"Do you think this matters, or is it just ancient history? Even her best friend Marsha didn't know."

"I think it could be important. One of the questions I was going to ask you, was if the artist's sketch resembled any male Kline family members. The DNA analysis showed that the killer's DNA had enough sequences similar to Beth's to suggest a familial relationship."

"When I showed it to her friends, Marsha thought he looked like Ben, but a decade younger. If you change the hairstyle and the eye color, there's a close resemblance. Do you think...the guy in the sketch...do you think it could be her son?"

"I don't know," Daniel said. "But I'll do my best to trace him and find out."

This could be the break he was looking for, or perhaps just another red herring. They were still checking out Jared. As soon as Hannah left, he'd phone Brenda with the information and see what the team could find out.

Hannah looked at him. "What was the other question you wanted to ask me?"

Daniel grinned. "One of my friends has the flu. He offered me two tickets tomorrow night to the LA Philharmonic. Any chance you could get a babysitter and come with me? They're performing Mozart."

"Well," Hannah said. "If it's Mozart, how can I refuse?"

CHAPTER FORTY-ONE

M Y DISCOVERY, AND SUBSEQUENT TALK WITH DANIEL, had left me agitated. I remembered how much Beth had loved children, and how excited she had been when I became pregnant.

When I finally left the office, I decided to take Zoe out for dinner. Her company always cheered me up. Zoe's dinner choices were predictable—cheese pizza, Sprite and chocolate frozen yogurt with rainbow sprinkles. I had a salad with walnuts, goat cheese and some kind of pasta with Thai chicken.

A pall of gloom surrounded me and I couldn't shake it. Even Zoe's adorable little face, covered in tomato sauce, didn't seem to help.

"Mommy," she said. "I'm worried about Aunt Beth."

I looked up, surprised. It had been six weeks, an eternity in the life of a four-year-old, and she hadn't mentioned Beth in a long time. Somehow, I'd thought she'd forgotten.

"What are you worried about, sweetheart?"

"When's she gonna find a new home up in the sky? When is she coming back down here?"

I put my fork down and reached out for her hand. "She can't come back down, honey. That's what it means when you die. She has to stay up there."

Her huge brown eyes stared up at me. Her mouth looked grim.

I was terrified she was going to ask me how Beth had died, and I hadn't formulated a good answer yet.

"You won't die, will you, Mommy?"

That one I could handle. "Of course not, sweetheart. I'll be with you till I'm very, very old."

She appraised me carefully. "You're not old Mommy—you're young."

I smiled at her. I felt like I was a-hundred-and-four.

Thank God for Zoe. From the moment she was born, she'd made everything in my life worthwhile.

I remembered the day I found out I was pregnant. Ben and I hadn't exactly been trying. Then again, we hadn't done much in the prevention department either. Like many yuppie, two income, professional couples without kids, we were ambivalent about starting a family. Even though my biological clock was rapidly approaching forty, neither of us was sure we wanted to trade our lifestyle in for sleepless nights, diapers, and PTA meetings.

Unlike differential diagnosis, this decision did not jump out at me from my medical books. Since I couldn't make up my mind, I kept forgetting my diaphragm. Ben kept forgetting to remind me. Neither of us wanted to take any real responsibility for a decision that awesome.

Even when my breasts became incredibly painful, and I

found myself unable to tolerate the smell of anything cooking, I was unsuspicious. It did, however, occur to me that, just to be thorough, I should run a pregnancy test.

When the stick turned blue, I was in shock. I couldn't figure out how to tell Ben. I finally left a bottle of prenatal vitamins on the dining room table.

Ben was always a quick study. He got it in two seconds, and I was astounded at the look of joy on his face.

He put his arms around me and swung me off the floor.

"I thought you were as ambivalent as I was."

He shook his head. "I didn't want to pressure you. I figured we'd have kids when you were ready. I've been ready for a while."

A stab of excitement hit me and started to build. It was a whole new project—new baby, new lifestyle—an organizational challenge worthy of my talents.

My pregnancy progressed perfectly and didn't slow me down a bit. My work schedule was horrendous, my appetite enormous, and my sex drive remarkably robust. I was busy demonstrating the latter to Ben one night, when he begged for mercy and rolled over, exhausted.

About halfway down his back I noticed a nasty-looking mole.

I gave him a week to make an appointment with the dermatologist, and then made it for him. Ben liked going to the doctor about as much as he liked setting his hair on fire. The doctor sent him home with a band-aid.

That was the last good day I remember. The next day, the dermatologist called Ben and told him it was melanoma. Two days later, he was in surgery, having a wide excision and a lymph node dissection. Two of the nodes were positive. The chemotherapy started the following week.

By October, I was six months pregnant, and Ben was beginning his second month of chemotherapy. He looked awful. His narrow face was positively gaunt, his lovely, thick, curly hair was falling out in handfuls, and his skin was sallow. Every time he'd go for a treatment, he'd spend the next three days at home, throwing up. I held his head, cleaned up after him, and murmured soothing platitudes that neither of us believed. I just prayed the chemotherapy would do some good, and be over soon.

Early in November, I had a paper accepted in the New England Journal, and came home early to share the news and to check on my husband. He'd been to the doctor earlier in the day, and I found him in the kitchen, head in hands, staring at the tabletop.

"I have good news and bad news," he said. "Which do you want to hear first?"

"Don't play games with me. Tell me what's wrong."

"The good news is, I don't need any more chemotherapy. The bad news is, it's metastasized to my lungs and liver, despite all the chemotherapy they gave me."

I couldn't say anything. I just held him tighter, tears streaming down my cheeks.

"We have to talk about it, honey," he said. "We don't have much time, and I need to be sure you and the baby will be okay without me."

"How can we possibly be okay without you? I love you. You can't die and leave me alone." By that time, I was crying uncontrollably, and Ben was holding me in his arms trying to comfort me.

"I'm sorry," I said. "I'm not making this any easier for you. I know you need to talk about it. How long do we have?"

"The doctor couldn't say exactly, but it's beginning to hurt every time I breathe. I don't know how long I'll be able to hold out without hospitalization. I'm hoping I can make it until the

baby comes. While we're sitting here, do you think we ought to decide on a name for that baby? I want to be sure you don't name her after me. Benjamin's a weird name for a girl. If it's all right with you, I'd like to call her Zoe."

Ben never made it to Zoe's birth. I woke up one morning, a few weeks later, to find him lying beside me, gasping for breath. I reached for the phone, called an ambulance and his doctor, who met us in the emergency room.

They attached Ben to an oxygen tank, and hooked him up to a morphine drip. In a few moments, I saw the lines of pain in his face relax, and his breathing ease.

He reached for my hand.

"I love you," he said, drifting into sleep, as the drug began to take effect.

Ben spent most of his time unconscious, his lucid periods fewer every day. I sat there, holding his hand and listening to him breathe, wanting to make sure I was there for him every time he had a conscious moment. The breathing grew slower, more like a snore, with wet gurgling sounds. We'd spent the previous few weeks saying goodbye. How many times can you tell someone you love them before you run out of words?

One night, I fell asleep in the chair by his bed. Something woke me suddenly, and I realized it was the silence. The tortured breathing had stopped, and the hand I'd been holding was cold.

"Mommy, it's time for dessert."

I snapped out of my reverie and focused on my child. Reaching across the table with a wet napkin, I wiped the pizza sauce from her face, and signaled the waitress for the check.

Zoe grinned at me. She had Ben's smile and it reminded

me once again that my glass really was half full. I'd had a wonderful marriage, and I have Zoe. Not everyone is that fortunate.

CHAPTER FORTY-TWO

T HE BRIGHT SPOT OF THE WEEK WAS MY SATURDAY date with Daniel, to attend the Los Angeles Philharmonic. One of the things we seemed to have in common, in addition to an addiction to mystery novels, was a love for classical music.

After the concert, we went to Rizzo's, an expensive downtown Italian restaurant in an exquisitely renovated art deco building. It was the sort of place Ben would have loved. In fact, we'd talked about going, but had never made it. Daniel and I had had dinner earlier, but the upstairs bar at Rizzos was an elegant treat. It had soft, cushioned banquettes, a small dance floor, and a pianist playing romantic music.

We ordered two glasses of champagne.

"Dance?" Daniel asked.

I nodded. He led me onto the floor and held me firmly against his chest. I'm a tall woman, but Daniel was substantially taller. His chin rested against my forehead as we moved in time to the music. I could feel one of his hands splayed out against my back. His arm brushed the side of my breast.

I took a deep breath, brought my hormones back under control, and smiled up at him. I hadn't done anything this romantic, with anyone, since Ben died.

Daniel held me against him, and bestowed a small kiss on my right index finger. The music seemed to get slower. It felt as if we were welded together.

"Was it difficult for you, raising Zoe alone, all these years?" he asked.

"Actually, Zoe's an easy child. I think it would have been harder for me without her."

He nodded. "No time for anyone else in your life?"

"There hasn't been," I said.

He drew me still closer and caressed my back with his fingers. Between us, pressing into my belly, I could feel him grow hard. His lips nuzzled my neck.

For the first time since Ben died, I felt alive below the waist. I wondered what he would feel like inside me—how it would be to run my fingers over that enticing bulge. The band chose that moment to take a break.

I followed Daniel back to our sofa and finished my drink.

He appraised me for a while, running a finger along my cheek. "Ready to go home?" he asked.

I nodded. What I didn't know was whether I was ready for what I was tempted to do when we got there.

I thanked Emilia for babysitting, watched her pull out of the driveway, and invited Daniel into the living room.

"Coffee?" I asked.

He shook his head. Somehow, I didn't think he'd want a Diet Coke either. He walked over to me, took my face in his hands and began kissing me.

His lips were surprisingly gentle. Somehow, I'd expected something more macho. *Me, Tarzan. You, Jane.* Followed by the two of us ripping each other's clothes off. He was giving me plenty of time to back out.

I let the pressure of his lips grow more intense, and slipped my arms around his neck. His tongue teased the edge of my mouth and I opened for him. It was a wonderful kiss.

My hormones were starting to rage again. His hands were on my breasts. His thumbs circled my nipples.

"Upstairs," I said.

He followed me up, unzipping my dress as we walked, pausing every few steps to pull me back against him and run his hands over my body. I didn't think we'd make it to the landing.

"I have to check on Zoe," I whispered, pointing down the hallway.

I turned on the light switch in my bedroom and motioned him to wait.

Zoe was sleeping like a little angel, all tangled in her blankets. I kissed her forehead and closed the door gently.

Daniel was waiting at the foot of my bed. He'd taken off his jacket and tie, and unbuttoned his shirt. I could see the dark hair curling on his chest. God, he was beautiful. I didn't love him, but I wanted him.

I wondered what the etiquette was for sex now. Did you both have to produce the results of your AIDS tests? Did everyone use condoms? Did Daniel have any on him? I certainly didn't.

We started to walk toward one other, when I caught

sight of Ben's silver-framed photo on my desk. It was like a splash of ice water.

Daniel turned and followed my gaze. "Ben?" he asked.

I nodded.

"You okay?"

"No," I said.

I could see his face harden. I could tell the moment had been ruined.

"I thought I was ready for this, but I'm not. It's got nothing to do with you, Daniel." I zipped my dress back up.

"Are you going to spend the rest of your life being faithful to a dead man?" he asked.

I didn't blame him for being pissed at me. I shouldn't have led him on. "I just can't handle anything intense right now. I'm sorry."

Daniel was buttoning his shirt, reaching for his jacket.

I'd probably never see him again.

He paused at the bedroom door. "After Annie left me, I wasn't ready for anything intense either. But I didn't put my life on hold. Ben won't come back, Hannah, and the odds are you won't find another man just like him. But you might find someone different, someone who could make you happy, if you gave yourself half a chance."

CHAPTER FORTY-THREE

DANIEL SLID INTO THE DRIVER'S SEAT OF HIS CAR AND slammed the door. He took a deep breath, battling both his sexual frustration and a profound sense of loss. He'd blown it. What a moron he was. He'd allowed himself to fall for a witness in a murder investigation, and he'd been stupid enough to try to seduce her, a mere six weeks after the murder. He should have known better.

He was sure he hadn't misread her excitement, or the passion in her response when she kissed him. Why hadn't he had the willpower to say goodnight, ask when he could see her again, and leave her wanting more? Instead, he'd moved too fast and ruined the whole thing.

She'd probably never want to be with him, at least not in his unprofessional capacity. He'd dated enough women, both before and after his divorce from Annie, to know how unique Hannah was. He didn't want to end things, but he was at a loss over what to do next.

With a sigh, he turned his key in the ignition and started for home.

CHAPTER FORTY-FOUR

I WATCHED DANIEL'S CAR PULL AWAY FROM THE CURB, feeling depressed and angry with myself. I'd ruined it. The only nice relationship I'd had with a man since Ben died five years ago, and I'd been too neurotic to move on with it. What was wrong with me? I'd wanted him. I liked him. Was I really planning to spend the rest of my life as a single martyr, mired in the deaths of my family members?

I couldn't decide if I wanted to cry or throw things. Every muscle in my body was in spasm. I needed a Valium or a massage. I needed an orgasm. I walked over to my desk and picked up Ben's photo.

"Is this how it's going to be?" I asked him. "Am I going to see your face every time I try to make love with another man?"

Ben didn't answer. The truth was that I knew he would want me to find someone else. We'd had such a wonderful marriage, so much love and laughter. If the situation had been reversed, I wouldn't have wanted him to spend the rest of his life in mourning. A marriage like ours was rare and special. I'd seen so many that hadn't come close to what we had. I thought about Beth, and the day she told me her marriage was ending.

It was a Sunday, one of those summer days that actually made you glad to be living in Los Angeles. I was doing workouts with weights, in front of the television, when the doorbell rang.

It was Beth, looking grim

"What's up?" I asked, as I opened the door.

"I'm leaving Josh. We're getting a divorce."

For a moment I was speechless. Then I took her in my arms, and gave her a long hug. "Oh, Beth, part of me wants to say how sorry I am, but most of me is just feeling immense relief."

"Me too," she said. "I should have done this a week after the wedding. Did you know I was his fifth wife? I didn't find that out until after we were married. He had a horrible temper. Everything had to be his way. He was so domineering, so opinionated. I tried desperately to make it work. For a while, I did everything he wanted, just to avoid fighting."

"I could tell how unhappy you were," I said.

"You could? But I never said anything to anyone."

"You didn't have to. It was obvious. I knew you wanted a baby, but I found myself hoping you wouldn't get pregnant with his child."

"Fat chance of that," she said. "I was willing to go through every infertility test in the book. He wouldn't even have a sperm count. Anyway, to get pregnant you have to have sex. One of his favorite methods of punishment was sexual withdrawal. I can't remember the last time we made love."

"What was the last straw?" I asked. "Why now?"

She shrugged. "We were having a huge fight this morning. About five minutes into it, I told him to hold the thought, and I went into my study and got my tape recorder. I switched it on and recorded the whole thing. He was so full of himself, so enchanted with hearing himself pontificate, he didn't even notice. If I'm ever tempted to go back to him, all I have to do is play it back."

"What can I do to help you?" I asked. "Would you like to stay here for a while, till you decide where you want to live?"

She shook her head. "Josh is going out of town tomorrow, for two weeks. That'll give me plenty of time to find a place to live and pack my things."

"I wish you'd told me earlier. Maybe, I could have helped."

"He said he'd divorce me, if I told anyone we were having problems."

"Do you need help looking for a place?" I asked. "There are lots of rentals in this neighborhood."

She hesitated. "I think I'm going to try to stay in Venice, near the synagogue."

"Are you sure you want to do that? Is the synagogue and this way of life really you, or is it just one more thing you did for him?"

She shook her head. "I don't know. I can't even begin to sort it out, till after he's out of my life. I'm just afraid to throw everything away at once. I need to take it one step at a time."

I conceded defeat. "Just be careful where in Venice you live," I said. "There are some areas that aren't too safe."

CHAPTER FORTY-FIVE

THE NEXT MORNING, AFTER MY ABORTED SEXUAL adventure, I took Zoe out for a carb-laden pancake breakfast. It was the least I could do—for myself. Drown my regrets from the night before, in maple syrup. Then, she and I made postpartum rounds at Memorial. My patients always found her adorable and the nurses made a fuss over her. After rounds, we headed for the playground, where Zoe exhausted herself and I read the Sunday papers.

When we got home, I fixed us both peanut butter and jelly sandwiches, and Zoe asked if she could go next door and play with Jennifer. In the peace and quiet of my empty house, I tried to decide what to do next. It had occurred to me that I still had Beth's journals in a cardboard box in my garage. I hadn't violated her privacy by reading them, and I hadn't yet decided whether to ship them to her parents. Perhaps one of them might hold a clue to her illegitimate son.

I opened the box, retrieved the volumes from 1990 and 1991, and began to read.

Sept 15th: Well, here I am in college. I'm sharing a room, half the size of mine at home, with a roommate. We've got bunk beds, and fortunately I drew the bottom one. Never liked heights. Roommate seems really sweet. I hope we'll get to be friends. I'm taking creative writing, psychology, French, and biology for non-science majors (my least favorite class). Creative writing looks quite promising. The professor is gorgeous.

Oct 10th: Got an A on my short story, with lots of flattering comments. I think Eric, my professor, really likes me. He's about forty, with the most penetrating dark eyes, a well-trimmed beard and a great body. His hair is long, but thinning a little on top, with just a hint of gray. It makes him look distinguished. Major crush.

Nov 16th : My writing skills are really improving. Eric is spending a lot of time with me in his office after hours. He says I am, by far, his most talented pupil. He thinks I have a real career as a writer in front of me. There is definitely some mutual chemistry there. He'll touch my hand or my shoulder when we are working, and I can feel a jolt of electricity between us. Yes, I know he's married, but I'm not looking for a husband. I'd just like to lose my virginity to someone experienced. How do I let him know I'm interested?

Dec 1st: Well, I figured it out. I wrote this erotic short story about a college student who has an affair with an older man. Just handed it in. We'll see.

Dec 5th: He got the message. I'm so glad. Now, I'm really a woman.

Dec 19th: Eric and I haven't been able to keep our hands off one another since this started. I'm crazy about him, about sex, about writing. It's all blended together in one ecstatic whole. Went to student health and got fitted for a diaphragm. It made me feel powerful and in control of my sexuality. I'll be finished with finals tomorrow and am actually feeling bummed-out that winter break is starting. I have to go home and Eric is going on vacation with his wife and kids. How can he stand to be with her, when he is obviously in love with me?

Feb 1st: Oh, God. I'm pregnant. I actually missed two periods before it hit me. Bought one of those pee tests at a pharmacy. It was positive. No wonder, I'm so nauseous. Part of me is actually thrilled. I'm carrying the child of the man I love. It must have happened the very first time. I'm going to have to tell him, but I'm scared. What if he won't leave her and marry me? I'll have to get an abortion and I have no idea of where to start.

March 30th: I haven't been able to write for weeks. I'm too depressed and panicked. I told Eric and he was awful. Told me he would never leave his wife. That this was my carelessness and my problem. He offered to pay for an abortion, but I'm already in my second trimester. I don't even know if I want an abortion. It would serve him right if I had his child and gave it away for adoption. I don't know what I'm going to do. I can't tell anyone, and I am fast running out of options. I certainly can't go home pregnant.

May 4th: Got into the University of Iowa's summer Creative Writing program. Told my parents that there wouldn't be time for me to come home before the program starts. I hope they don't have an irresistible parental impulse to visit me over the summer. I'm five months along now and can actually feel the baby move. I've bought a bunch of those loose tie-dye tops and bigger jeans. I don't think anyone has noticed yet. My friends probably just think I've gained the Freshman fifteen.

July 8th: Iowa is hot and humid, but the program is really interesting. I'd be having a good time, if I wasn't pregnant and scared to death. I signed up for the obstetrics clinic at the county hospital and they connected me with an adoption agency. I don't see that I have a choice. I certainly can't support a kid. It would destroy college and any chance I have of being a real writer. Only two more months and it will be over, and I can go home. I swear, I will never get involved with a married guy again.

Sept 5th: I had a baby boy, and it hurt like hell. I wouldn't let them give me any medication. I deserve the pain. I deserve to be punished. I didn't look at the baby or touch him. The nurse took him away, as soon as they cleaned him up and made sure he was breathing. I didn't want to see what he looked like. I was afraid, if I held him, I wouldn't be able to go through with it. I just hope he gets loving parents and a better life than I could have given him.

By the time I finished the journal entry, tears were streaming down my face. My heart ached for her. How could she have carried this secret with her to the grave? It explained so much. Why hadn't she confided in Ben? He would have helped her. I know he would have. I wondered what I would have done in her place. There had to be a way to trace Beth's son. I knew what Daniel suspected, but he could be wrong. Perhaps Beth's son was a brilliant, talented, kind man who could give some comfort to her parents. First thing on Monday morning, I was going to call Iowa.

CHAPTER FORTY-SIX

T HE FIRST ITEM, ON DANIEL'S MONDAY STAFF MEETING
agenda, was Beth's brother Jared.

"Dead end," Brenda said. "We checked the mileage on his car and he certainly didn't drive it to LA. In fact, I doubt he took it anywhere but the airport and back, and to alternate casinos. He didn't fly to LA, either. We have security tapes from the Bellagio showing him playing poker at midnight on Sunday, so he's got a perfect alibi. Incidentally, he's a regular at the Bellagio. He seems to have a little gambling addiction and he loses a lot of money. The guy has a perfect motive, but also an unbreakable alibi. I suppose, he could have hired someone to do the deed."

"You're forgetting the DNA," Daniel said. "Whoever killed her was related to her. We need to get hold of the Iowa adoption records on Beth's son. At the moment, it seems like the only viable investigative channel."

"You think this guy Randy could be her son?" Brenda asked.

"I think it's possible, unless his resemblance to Hannah's deceased husband is just the result of poor memory by a witness, and an inaccurate drawing by our artist. In any case, Beth's son is the only missing male family member, so we have to track him down."

"How are you planning to get hold of sealed adoption records from another state?" someone else asked.

"I'm going to present our evidence to a prosecutor with a brain, and ask for a subpoena. If they fight it, we'll go a Federal judge. Whatever it takes," Daniel said. "I take it no one has managed to find Randy?"

Silence greeted him.

"Okay, that's it for this morning. I'm going to go over my list of prosecutors and decide who's the best bet."

CHAPTER FORTY-SEVEN

I PHONED THE IOWA ADOPTION AGENCY, INTRODUCED myself as Dr. Kline, and asked for the director. The doctor title usually got cooperation, regardless of whom you called.

When I had her on the phone, I explained my errand. A relative, Beth Kline, had recently died. I knew that she had given up a child for adoption through their agency, and was attempting to trace him. I felt obligated to inform him of the death of his birth mother, as he was her only heir.

There was something about the word *heir* that made people sit up and take notice. The director put me on hold while she checked the files.

"We heard from Beth Kline just this past year," she said. "We sent a letter with her contact information to her son, at his adoptive parent's last known address. I don't know if contact was ever made."

"Given the circumstances, could you possibly give me the address? It would be of great benefit to him."

I could feel her hesitation, but finally, she relented. "If

you can fax me a copy of Beth Kline's death certificate, as well as your identification, I can give you the information."

I took her fax number, and gave her my office and cell phones.

Then, I retrieved the death certificate and headed for my office fax machine. I wanted to send her the information before she had a chance to change her mind.

CHAPTER FORTY-EIGHT

D ANIEL HUNG UP THE PHONE IN FRUSTRATION, AND BIT into the stale tuna sandwich he'd purchased from the police vending machine. He washed it down with equally bad coffee. He'd selected a prosecutor he'd liked, and had worked with extensively, only to find that his choice was tied up in court.

Daniel left a message for him to call, as soon as he returned to his office, and busied himself in paperwork from other cases. He was closing in. He could feel it, and he had Hannah to thank for it. She'd supplied all the best information. But thinking about her just increased his frustration.

He was in a thoroughly bad mood when his cell rang. "Ross here."

"It's Hannah. I just learned something you need to know."

"Hannah, I'm so glad you called. What is it?"

"It's Beth's son. His name is Randall Watkins, and his adopted parents are Isobel and Alan Watkins. Here's their last known address."

Daniel picked up his pen and wrote down the information. "Are you going to tell me how you managed to get sealed adoption records?"

"I just called the director, told her Beth had died and her son was the heir to the estate. She was cautious enough to ask for documentation, but once I sent it, she phoned me with the information."

"You are an amazing woman. You're better than a subpoena. In fact, I was just waiting for a prosecutor to call me back so I could request one. Have you ever considered a career in law enforcement?"

"Not a chance," Hannah said.

"Look, I owe you an apology for last night," Daniel started.

"You don't owe me anything, Daniel. It was just bad timing, honestly. If anything, I'm the one who should apologize. I really do like you and I didn't mean to hurt your feelings. Please don't take it personally."

"Any chance we could forget about it and take things at a pace you can handle? I think you're special and I'm not in a hurry."

"That's the nicest thing anyone's said to me in a long time. It's a deal. Will you keep me posted on what you find out?"

"I will, I promise. Any chance of dinner next weekend?"

"Absolutely," Hannah said.

Daniel let out a relieved breath. It looked as if he hadn't blown it after all. "That would be great. I'll call you in a few days and we'll pick a time and place. In the meantime, I'm going to see what I can find out about the Watkins family."

CHAPTER FORTY-NINE

DANIEL PHONED ON THURSDAY, AND WE MADE A dinner date for Saturday night. He hadn't found Beth's son yet, but he had learned a few things. He promised to share them, when we saw one another.

I asked him to pick me up at home a little early. I'd decided it was time for him to spend a few minutes with Zoe. My daughter seemed to have very good instincts when it came to people. She was very picky about her friends, and they were all sweet, well-behaved kids. I wanted to see how she reacted to Daniel, and vice versa.

I greeted him at the door, experiencing, once again, that flash of desire that disconcerted me. He was wearing jeans, and a blue sweater that matched the color of his eyes. He gave me a chaste kiss on the cheek and I drew him into the den, where Zoe was engrossed in a book.

"Zoe," I said, "This is my friend Daniel. We're going out to dinner."

Zoe looked up.

Daniel smiled and bent down, so that the two of them were at eye level. "Hello Zoe. I've been looking forward to seeing you. Your mom talks about you all the time."

Zoe favored him with a shy smile.

"What are you reading?" Daniel asked, seating himself opposite her.

Zoe held out *The Giving Tree*.

"I remember that book. I read it as a child, but I don't think I could read it by myself, at your age. You must be pretty smart."

Zoe nodded. "I am. I just learned to read. This is my first book."

"I'm impressed," Daniel said. "It's kind of a sad story, don't you think?"

"I think it's sad and happy," Zoe said. "Do you like Ninja Turtles?"

"I've never watched them," Daniel confessed. "What are they about?"

I went upstairs to my bedroom, to retrieve my purse and a shawl, and to tell Emilia that I wouldn't be home too late. When I got back, the two of them were playing with Zoe's Ninja action figures. It looked like a good start to me.

I kissed the top of her head. "Can I have Daniel back?" I asked. "I'm hungry."

"Sure, Mommy. Have a nice dinner," Zoe said.

———

Daniel held the passenger door of his car open for me and I slipped in.

"I didn't make reservations," he said. "I thought we'd go somewhere casual in the neighborhood."

"That's fine with me. Any chance we could go to the place where Beth spent her last night?" I asked. "I know it seems crazy, but I feel like I need to see it. I'm not sure why. Some kind of closure, perhaps."

"It's called CJ's," Daniel said. "It's pretty noisy, but we can go there if you really want to."

"I do," I confirmed.

———

CJ's served gourmet beers and flavored margaritas. We ordered some spicy olives, guacamole, a raspberry margarita for me and a beer for Daniel, and waited for our entrees. I was hungry. I was also anxious. I hadn't expected, nor deserved, an apology from Daniel, and I was relieved that he hadn't seemed angry. In fact, he'd been incredibly nice about it all. Maybe I hadn't totally ruined it, but I wasn't quite sure of how to proceed.

"You seem to have made a hit with Zoe," I said, as I dug into my tostada. "She doesn't let just anyone play with her Ninja Turtles."

"Glad to hear it," Daniel said. "I have a niece and a nephew, so I've had some practice." He bit into a rare hamburger.

"Tell me what's going on with the investigation, Daniel? Did you find out anything new?" Fair was fair. I'd given him major information. I expected quid pro quo.

"I did," he said. "Isobel Watkins still lives at the same address. She's been divorced from her husband for ten years. He's spent most of that time in prison for armed robbery, and he's still there."

"Sounds like the adoption agency picked the wrong family," I said. "What a tragedy. Did you trace the son?"

"I haven't found him yet, but I did find some useful information. He dropped out of high school and has a juvenile record. Sealed, of course. There's no adult record, listed phone or driver's license. He's not on social media. So, I called his mother's phone number and asked for Randall. She said he didn't live with her any longer. I told her I was a Los Angeles estate attorney, trying to locate her adopted son because his birth mother had passed away and left him money. You'd done so well with that approach, I thought I'd try it."

"Did it work?"

"She believed me. I could hear the greed kick in on the phone, but she claimed not to know where he was. She said he'd been living at home, freeloading, since he dropped out of school. A couple of months ago, he helped himself to her cash supply, packed a duffel, and said he was leaving, that there was someone he wanted to look up. She claimed not to know where he was going. Apparently, he hitchhiked. Doesn't have a car or a cell phone."

"Do you think he came here?"

"I do," Daniel said. "We traced the man who had spoken to Beth at CJ's, the night she died. We were able to find out that he'd stayed in the Venice Community Homeless Shelter, and that his name was Randy. We've been searching for Randy all over Venice and Santa Monica, for weeks. I find it hard to believe that the man we've been looking for, whose police drawing resembles your husband, isn't Randall Watson."

"Tell me the truth, Daniel. Do you honestly think that Beth's son murdered her?"

Daniel took a while to answer, and his eyes were sad. "I can't come up with an alternate solution," he said. "You're a physician, so you probably understand DNA evidence better than I do. It's clear that her assailant was a close male relative. All her other male relatives have unbreakable alibis."

I buried my face in my hands and took a deep breath. When I looked up, I was sure my eyes were wet. "Poor Beth. Every effort she made to do the right thing backfired. Why would he have wanted to kill her? It doesn't make sense."

"Sometimes, there are no good answers."

We finished our meal, lost in thought, and Daniel signaled for the check. The restaurant was just beginning to fill with noisy twenty-somethings.

"Let's take a walk," he said.

I nodded, grateful for the thought of fresh air.

We began to stroll south on Main Street, and then into Venice, along Abbott Kinney Boulevard. I should have been paying more attention to where I was walking, but I was too busy looking at Daniel. Klutz that I am, I tripped in a pothole, landing on my hands and knees.

"Hannah, are you hurt?" Daniel bent down, holding out his hands to help me up.

I was hurt, actually. My hands were bloody and both knees burned like hell. If I hadn't been wearing slacks, they'd have been scraped raw.

I hadn't done anything like this in years. In fact, the last time I'd fallen had been in the Harvard bookstore, the day I met Ben. I wondered if this was a sign.

"I don't think anything's broken. Let me see if I can get up." I grabbed his arms for leverage, and slowly pulled myself into a standing position.

But when I tried to walk, I limped.

Daniel put his arm around me, and guided me to a bus stop bench at the corner. Then, he pulled a pack of tissues from his pocket and mopped up the blood on my hands.

"Why don't you wait here Hannah? I'll run back and bring the car."

It sounded like a good plan to me.

He turned, and started walking rapidly back toward the parking lot.

I rolled up my pants and assessed the damage to my knees. I was feeling heartbroken. I almost wished that I hadn't gotten involved and discovered the key to the murder. Perhaps it would have been better never to know.

Poor Beth. To have wanted a child so badly, to have given away the only one you ever had, and then to be murdered by your own son. It was beyond thinking. I kept asking myself *why*, but I couldn't find any answers.

Tears began to drip uncontrollably down my cheeks. I blew my nose with a tissue, and wiped my eyes with my sleeve. Then, I looked back along Abbot Kinney to see if I could spot Daniel's car. All I could see was a shabbily dressed young man, carrying a backpack, and walking in my direction. There was something familiar about him.

I tensed as he approached me.

"Hey lady, can you spare a few bucks? I haven't eaten since yesterday."

I looked up, startled to find myself gazing into a pair of cold green eyes and a narrow face. A face that I had seen before, and not just in a police sketch. In my mind, I visualized Beth, coming out of a convenience store on Main Street, walking toward me, handing a dollar to a bearded homeless man. This man was clean-shaven, but I recognized the eyes.

He was Randall Watkins. I was sure of it.

CHAPTER FIFTY

MY HEART WAS POUNDING. I WAS STARTING TO FEEL nauseous and clammy. I was scared. This guy was almost certainly Beth's son. And her killer.

I had to keep him talking until Daniel got here.

"I think I can spare some money," I said, smiling sweetly. "No fun being hungry."

I reached into my purse, fumbled for my wallet without removing it, and pulled out the first bill I could get my hands on. It was a twenty.

I handed it to him.

"Thanks, lady. Most people don't give more than a buck."

"I don't think a buck would buy you much in the way of food," I said. "Are you homeless?"

He shrugged. "Haven't been here very long. Jobs and cheap beds are hard to find."

"Where are you from?" I asked.

"Midwest. I like the weather here better. Do you live close by? You wouldn't happen to have a spare room I could sleep in?"

Did he really expect me to take him home with me? I shuddered at the thought.

"Sorry," I said. "I'm just an out-of-town tourist. There might be some homeless shelters in Santa Monica."

He shrugged. "Hey, your hands are bleeding."

"I know. I caught my foot in a pothole and fell." I fished in my purse for Daniel's tissues.

"I could walk you to your hotel," he suggested.

This was getting creepy. Fortunately, I spotted Daniel's Mustang at the red light, a block away.

"That's really sweet of you to offer," I said, "but a friend is picking me up in a few minutes. Good luck," I added.

He didn't seem to get the hint, because he didn't move.

Daniel's car pulled up at the bus stop.

I got up, opened the passenger door, and gave Randall a cheery wave.

"Thank God, you're here," I said, getting in and locking the door. "That panhandler I was talking to is Randall Watson."

"Are you sure?"

Hannah nodded. "I recognized him. I saw him, down the street from her apartment, just hours before she was killed."

CHAPTER FIFTY-ONE

WATSON HAD FINALLY GIVEN UP ON HANNAH, AND was walking in the direction of Main Street. After half a block, he seated himself in the doorway of a closed boutique.

Daniel parked his car at the bus stop, and put his police sticker on the dashboard. Then he took out his cell and requested backup.

"Stay in the car and keep it locked," he told Hannah.

"Daniel, you aren't armed," Hannah said.

"Yeah, I am," he said. "Haven't you ever heard of martial arts?"

"Daniel! I don't want you to get hurt."

"If it is Watkins, I'll have to arrest him. I may not get another chance, before he disappears again."

Daniel walked rapidly up the street and approached the panhandler.

"You Randy?" he asked.

"Who wants to know?" the man asked.

Daniel pulled out his ID. "Police," he said. "Are you Randall Watkins?"

"Okay, yeah. I know, I shouldn't be panhandling. I'll move."

"Can I see some ID?" Daniel asked.

"I don't have any ID."

"But you say you're Randall Watkins?"

"Yeah, so what?"

"So, I'm going to have to ask you to come with me. We've been looking for you. You're a witness in a case we're working on."

The man sprung up, as if getting ready to run, but Daniel had him on the ground and in a hammerlock before he took a step.

Two police cars arrived within minutes.

"Cuff him and take him in," Daniel said. "Book him for panhandling. I'll be in to question him within half an hour. Oh, and you might feed him while he's waiting."

One of the patrolmen cuffed Watkins and put him in the back seat of a patrol car.

Daniel returned to Hannah. "I'm afraid I'm going to have to cut our evening short. I'll drive you home and then head to the station. You were right. He is Randall Watkins."

When Daniel entered the interview room, Watkins was finishing off a hamburger, with fries and a large coke. Brenda sat opposite him, quietly observing. There was a tape recorder beside her, but it wasn't running.

"Hello, Randy, I'm Detective Ross," Daniel said. "Was dinner okay?"

Watkins shrugged. "Not bad for police food. So, what's this about? What am I supposed to be a witness to?"

Daniel flipped on the recorder. "If you don't object, I want to record this, so I don't forget anything you say."

"Are you accusing me of something?"

"Not yet," Daniel said. "You were found panhandling, which is a misdemeanor, but that isn't what this interview is about."

Daniel figured he'd start slow, get Watkins to relax. He didn't have to read him his rights until he arrested him for murder, but he wanted to get as much information as possible before that.

Of course, he was going to have to charge him with murder before the interview was over. It was the only way to get his DNA sample. Even though Watkins' DNA was all over his dinner leftovers, Daniel didn't think he could hold him until the specimen or results came back, and it had taken long enough to find him. He couldn't risk the guy running and vanishing again.

"What do you want to know?"

"Let's start with a few basics," Daniel said. "Can you state your name, your age and where you were born?"

"Randy Watkins. I'm twenty and I'm from Iowa."

"Date of birth?"

"September 5th, 1991."

"So, Randy, what brought you to California?"

"The weather. You ever spend a winter in Iowa?"

"Can't say as I have," Daniel said. "When did you get here?"

"I've been here about two months."

"Did you drive from Iowa?"

"Nah, don't have a car. I hitched."

"What's your address?"

"Don't have one. I've been living on the streets and in shelters. The homeless guys said Santa Monica was real generous with meals and there were lots of good shelters at this end of town. I've been looking for a job, but no luck so far."

"Is that why you were panhandling?"

"Gotta have a little cash, don't I?"

"You know anyone in LA?" Daniel asked.

"Nope, just the guys I met in the shelter."

"So, you didn't plan to stay with a friend or relative when you got here? There was no one you wanted to look up?"

"I just said so, didn't I?"

"Randy, a few weeks ago, you went to a restaurant called CJ's. For a beer, is that right?"

"Is it a crime to have a beer?"

"Were you at CJ's?"

"Yeah, what of it?"

"Did you try to pick up a woman while you were there?"

"I may have. She wasn't interested. What difference does it make?"

"You may have been the last person to see her alive. She was murdered that night."

"What's that got to do with me? You think I did it?"

Daniel paused. It was time. "Actually, Randall, I do. I'm arresting you for the murder of Beth Kline, your birth mother. You have the right to remain silent and the right to ask for an attorney."

"You'd better believe I want an attorney. I'm not saying one more damn thing."

CHAPTER FIFTY-TWO

DANIEL CALLED ME THAT NIGHT, TO TELL ME THAT Watkins had been charged with Beth's murder.

"Are you sure it was him?" I asked.

"I'll be certain when the DNA specimen comes back and is compared to the DNA under Beth's nails. That's the definitive piece of evidence. But, everything else fits. He's not talking yet, but when I can confront him with the evidence, maybe he'll confess."

Daniel phoned again, a week later, to tell me that the DNA was a match, and that Watkins arraignment was scheduled for the following week. He was being charged with first-degree murder.

"So, it's over," I said.

"Until the trial."

"I'm relieved. Maybe now, I can stop obsessing about it. Daniel, is there any way to keep this from Beth's parents? Their hearts are already broken. I don't know what this will do to them."

"If it were up to me to prosecute, I would make a case about a panhandler who stalked her and followed her home from a bar. But the defense will use the information that he was her abandoned son, to try to win the sympathy of the jury. Unless her parents choose not to follow any of the media during the trial, they're bound to find out."

"That means, I have to tell them." One more horrible chore. "I appreciate everything you've done to solve this, Daniel."

"I couldn't have solved it without you, and that's the truth, Hannah. Your insights and information were invaluable. We're a good team."

"Thanks, but I'm not planning on a career in law enforcement."

"I know," Daniel said. "You already have a day job. One more thing, Hannah. We can't see one another again, at least, not until the trial is over. There's a reason detectives aren't supposed to date witnesses in cases they're investigating. The defense could use that information to imply collusion between us, in our testimony. I can't risk doing anything that could jeopardize a conviction in this case."

"I didn't realize you weren't supposed to date me. Why did you?"

"You were irresistibly attractive. You still are. I wasn't thinking with my cop-brain, when I asked you to dinner."

"It wasn't a date," I said. "You were continuing to question an important witness, who insisted on seeing the place where Beth had spent her final hours. I was afraid to go there by myself."

"Right," Daniel said.

"It's a good thing we haven't gone to bed," I added.

"Yet," Daniel said.

CHAPTER FIFTY-THREE

ALLING MY IN-LAWS, AND TELLING THEM THE TRUTH about Beth's death, was the hardest thing I'd ever done. They were devastated, angry, disbelieving and depressed. The family phone calls that followed for weeks afterwards wore me down. It was close to impossible to maintain the façade of cheerful Mommy for Zoe, and calm, competent doctor for all my demanding patients.

Andrea went so far as to suggest therapy and an antidepressant, but I refused. I didn't have time for therapy, and I didn't want to rely on drugs. I would just have to deal with all of this, my own way.

To make matters worse, I found myself missing Daniel. Until he was gone, I hadn't realized what a reassuring presence he had been in my life. He'd said "until after the trial," but who knew if he really meant it? He was probably dating some hot blonde and had forgotten all about me.

The trial began in September and lasted three weeks. I didn't go to all of it. The last thing I wanted to do was to see pictures of Beth's murdered body. I was called to testify about Beth's last afternoon and my discovery of her illegitimate son. I described finding his birth certificate and a letter from the adoption agency in Beth's safety deposit box. I didn't mention her journals. Those were private. No one asked me anything about Daniel.

The only other testimony I went to court for was that of the defendant. His attorney had placed him on the stand, hoping for a second-degree conviction. Randall had testified to his upbringing by an abusive father who "beat the shit out of him," and an alcoholic mother. He didn't learn he was adopted, until he received a letter from the agency with Beth Kline's contact information.

He was stunned and angry. The thought that he'd been abandoned, and given to adoptive parents like the Watkins, infuriated him. At first, he didn't want anything to do with Beth, but then he decided to meet her, to see what kind of a person she was and what she might have to offer him. He had nothing to lose.

He hitchhiked to Los Angeles and located her. He followed her around for several weeks, learning her routines, and trying to decide when and where to approach. He'd trailed her to CJ's and decided to introduce himself.

"She blew me off, didn't even look at me," he'd testified.

She'd driven herself home, but he knew where she lived, and tried the back door. It was open. She had heard him come into the kitchen and started to scream. He yelled at her that he was her son. She refused to believe him. He'd been enraged, grabbed a knife from the counter, dragged her into the bedroom and started stabbing.

The defense argued that it was a crime of passion. The prosecutor pointed out that he'd been stalking her for weeks. The jury went with the prosecution. Randall Watkins was convicted of first-degree murder. He was sentenced to life in prison without parole.

I wondered what Beth would have thought of the sentence. I couldn't begin to imagine what that last night had been like for her. Finally finding her son, and the pain of recognizing that he was nothing like the boy she must have imagined. The horror when he broke into her apartment and stabbed her to death.

Despite the verdict, I was still feeling as if I were functioning on empty. The sense of anticlimax was overwhelming. I hadn't been interested in anything since the trial had ended.

The question I was struggling with was, *what was I going to do now for me*?

I'd spent the past six months living Beth's life by proxy. I'd cleaned up her messes, delved into her most intimate secrets, and befriended her friends. I'd spent the previous five years mourning Ben, and devoting myself to the office and to Zoe.

In a few years, Zoe would have better things to do than play with Mommy. Maybe it was finally time to start living my own life.

I took a deep breath, gathered my courage, picked up the phone and dialed.

"Detective Ross please. It's Dr. Kline calling."

"Hannah. I'm so glad to hear from you. How are you?"

"I'm holding it together," I said. "I'm glad the trial is finally over."

"Not as glad as I am," he said.

"Any chance we could get together for dinner?" I asked. "I don't think I'm a witness any longer."

"I'd love to," Daniel said. "You have no idea of the willpower I've had to exert to avoid calling you over the past few months. How about you come to my house and I'll cook for you. I'm not bad with a barbecue."

"Sounds great," I said. "I'll bring the wine."

I couldn't believe I'd actually done that.

CHAPTER FIFTY-FOUR

D ANIEL'S HOUSE WAS ON ONE OF THOSE CHARMING pedestrian streets, just off the beach. It had probably been someone's summer bungalow in the 1940s. It was made of wood siding, painted white with blue trim, and had a small front yard with a white picket fence, and lots of flowerpots on the front porch.

The inside was small and sparsely furnished. It had probably been remodeled when he was married to Annie. I noticed white walls, polished dark wood floors, a few Navaho rugs and a brown leather sofa.

"All single men have brown leather furniture," Andrea had informed me, back when she was still dating.

At least, Daniel's was in excellent taste.

He deposited me on the sofa and disappeared into the kitchen with my cold bottle of Sauvignon Blanc. I heard the pop of a cork, and he reappeared with two cold glasses of wine and a tray with Brie, crackers and grapes.

I spread a cracker, bit into it, and sipped the wine slowly.

"It's been a rough few weeks for you," Daniel said.

I reached for another cracker.

"Does it help?" he asked. "Finally having her killer put away for good?"

"I don't know. It helps not to have to ask myself the same questions, over and over again, but now that I know the answers, I don't know what to do with them. She was so unhappy. It breaks my heart. She never told anyone. But, she could have told me. I would have understood. I wouldn't have judged."

"I know you wouldn't have," Daniel said.

He put his wine glass down on the coffee table and moved a little closer to me.

"It's okay to cry about it," he said. "It might help."

I wasn't sure I needed to cry. Maybe it would be better to scream and throw things. My rage and frustration mingled with the pain.

Daniel drew me to him, putting his arms around me, and pressing my head gently onto his shoulder. I relaxed onto his chest like a deflated balloon, felt his kisses on my forehead, the kind of kisses I always give Zoe, when she skins her knee.

I don't know how long we sat there, holding one another, when I realized I wanted him to make love to me, or when I understood that he wasn't going to make the first move. I'd never had to seduce a man before, but I thought I could improvise.

I drew back, looking at him, and touched his face lightly with the tips of my fingers. "You've been a real friend, Daniel. Thank you. I've missed you."

I leaned over and brushed his lips with my mouth, waiting to be certain he wouldn't pull away, before increasing the pressure and allowing him to see I wanted a real kiss.

I heard his breathing quicken and felt his arms tighten around me.

I slid my hands down along his chest and up again, under his sweater. The skin on his back was warm and smooth. I stroked it, came around his waist and explored the coarse hair on his chest.

He extricated himself from me long enough to take off both our shirts.

I undid my bra.

He lowered me onto the leather sofa, covering me with the full length of his body. The leather felt cold against my back, his chest warm and fuzzy against my nipples. I located his buttocks with both hands and pulled them toward me, arching against him, feeling the confirmation I was looking for.

"Are you sure you're ready, Hannah?" he whispered into my ear.

I answered by turning my mouth to kiss him, moving my thigh against the length of his erection.

His mouth slid along the side of my neck, took a detour to my breast, and came to rest at the waistband of my jeans. His fingers stroked the rough denim covering my inner thighs and between them. I felt as if I were dissolving, soaking through my clothes.

I reached between his legs to reciprocate.

"This might work better with fewer layers," he said.

I nodded.

He stood up and discarded the remainder of his things. His body lived up to its promise, tanned and muscular, dark hairs mingling with gray.

I unzipped my jeans and he helped me wriggle out of them.

I held out my arms to him and he knelt beside me, one hand stroking my cheek, the other buried in the wetness between my legs, watching my face, as I gave into the sensuality I'd abandoned five years ago.

He was experienced. I could tell by the way his hand read my body's nonverbal signals. It felt like he'd been making love to me for years, except for the excitement, which kept increasing between us, until I felt like I could barely breathe.

I urged him on top of me and drew him inside me, wrapping my legs tightly around his hips. I held him, feeling his deft strokes, meeting each one of them with an eagerness I hadn't realized I still possessed.

And then, at the moment I felt him orgasm, felt my own pelvis begin to contract in waves of pleasure, I opened my eyes and saw an expression of love, starkly revealed on his face.

I continued to see Daniel. We made love at his house, and eventually, at mine, but neither of us ever stayed overnight. We took Zoe on family outings to the museum, the park, and pancake breakfasts. We were taking it slow, but it felt healing.

I thought I was ready for a next step.

Once again, I picked up the phone.

"Hi. I'll bet you were calling to see if I was free for lunch," Daniel said.

"Not a chance," I said. "I've got surgery all day. I was actually calling to see if you were free for a little vacation. I need a beach, some sunshine, a mystery novel and some good company. Not necessarily in that order."

There was a long pause on the telephone.

"You've stunned me into silence," he said. "Why don't I stop by the travel agent, pick up some brochures, and we can discuss it tonight?"

"You're on," I said.

EPILOGUE
ONE MONTH LATER

"WHAT'S THE MATTER, MOMMY? ARE YOU SAD?" ZOE asked.

I'd been looking at the calendar. I glanced down and ran my fingers over her long curly hair. "I was just thinking that today is Aunt Beth's birthday. I guess I do feel sad. I still miss her a lot."

"Is she gonna have a party up in the sky?" Zoe asked.

"I don't know, sweetheart. Maybe people do have birthday parties after they die, I just don't know."

"I want Aunt Beth to have a party," Zoe said.

When I got home that evening, Zoe was frosting a chocolate cake, and Daniel was waiting with our plane tickets to Charleston.

He took me into his arms and deposited a kiss on my forehead. "Do I get to sample the cake?" he asked Zoe.

She gave him one of her more enchanting smiles.

It occurred to me, that this was the first time she'd had a man in her life. I liked watching them together.

"Emilia and I made it for Aunt Beth," she said. "We have to light candles and all sing 'Happy Birthday'."

I bent down and took her into my arms. She looked so proud of herself, and the cake looked great.

"I'll get the candles, "I said.

I didn't have forty-two candles, so we settled for six and I lit a match.

"Happy Birthday to you. Happy Birthday to you," Zoe sang in her small piping voice. "Do you think she can hear me, Mommy?"

"I'm sure she can, sweetheart. I'll bet that, up in the sky, Aunt Beth can even eat chocolate cake without getting zits on her face."

Daniel reached for my hand and I let myself relax against his chest.

"Happy Birthday, Beth," I whispered. "Wherever you are."

ACKNOWLEDGMENTS

Many people contributed to this effort. My stalwart editor and writing teacher, Linda Schreyer, gave me her wisdom, her friendship and her apt commentary. Cathy Novak, my writing class buddy, shared her pithy observations. I am also indebted to the other members of my writing retreat group, Darlene, Erica and Jackie, for their feedback.

My brother-in-law, Jerry Bernstein, a criminal defense attorney, allowed me to pick his brain on issues of adoption and DNA sampling. My husband Uri, as always, has been my IT guru and first reader.

My new publisher, Christiana Miller of Third Street Press, did a stellar job with a second round of edits, and Dan Van Oss designed the new cover and made my vision of Hannah real.

I am deeply grateful to all of "Beth's" many friends, who generously gave of their time and insight, in helping me to fully understand who she was and how she affected those around her. When she died, the world lost a very special woman.

AUTHOR BIO

 PAULA BERNSTEIN is a physician, a scientist, and the author of the Hannah Kline Mystery Series. Like her main character, Paula has spent her professional career as a practicing obstetrician gynecologist. In addition to her medical mystery series, her short story, *On Call for Murder,* was published in *LAst Resort,* the 2017 Sisters in Crime Anthology. Her website is www.HannahKlineMysteries.com.

ALSO BY PAULA BERNSTEIN

The Hannah Kline Mysteries

Murder in the Family

Murder by Lethal Injection

Murder in a Private School

Murder in the Goldilocks Zone

Short Stories

Potpourri

Made in the USA
Monee, IL
21 May 2022